I0778943

JEREMY JAE JAE DAVIS

Merie Vision Publishing
Merievisionpublishing@gmail.com

ISBN: 978-1-961213-16-6

Library of Congress control number on record

Formatting and Editing by
Merie Vision Publishing, LLC

Printed in the United States of America

MASKED :

THE RISE

OF

JACKHAMMER

SLIM

BOOK 2

CHAPTER 1

The coliseum arena was packed to capacity with over 4,100 women screaming at the top of their lungs as Jackhammer Slim graced the stage with style, grace, and perfection. He noticed a beautiful woman standing in the audience wearing an, I'm in love with Jackhammer Slim t-shirt. He pointed in her direction and had his security escort her to the stage. For a few seconds, she stood in shock until her girlfriends began nudging her forward. She couldn't believe this was happening. While covering her mouth in awe, she began walking and finally made it to the big stage. That's when The World-Famous Jackhammer Slim took her hand, kissed it, and sat her down in his exclusive red velvet chair. He bumped, grind, and wined all over her body for two minutes straight.

Overwhelmed with a burst of emotions, out of instinct, the woman reached for his mask. Everyone knew that was against house rules. So, like the gentleman he is, he professionally removed her hand, but she continued tugging at his mask determined to see his face. That's when he knew he had to hurry and wrap his set.

Within a matter of seconds, he signaled for his security and gracefully had the woman escorted back to her seat. This was one of many acts he performed nightly. He loved engaging with his audience. Even though the risk factors were high, he still felt the need to give the fans a more intimate version of Jackhammer Slim.

Las Vegas, Nevada

The six-bedroom, eight-bathroom,13,489 square foot, 15.8-million-dollar estate was located at 27 Eagles Landing Ln, Las Vegas, Nevada. Standing in his foyer admiring his overwhelming catalog of accolades. Rico's road to success wasn't a walk in the park, but looking back, he knew his journey was well worth it. He'd been entertaining at the Caesars Palace venue for over five years when the original Jackhammer Slim, aka James Saunders, retired and passed him the torch. Since then, success has found favor in him.

He'd also been through an ugly custody battle with the mother of his two children, Tamia. She wasn't mentally strong enough to deal with his career of being an exotic dancer. Tamia and his two children were living at their grandparent's home in Chesapeake. Two weekends a month, he would fly back home to Virginia to visit and spoil them rotten. He still loved Tamia without a doubt, and every visit before he would leave, he assured her that she had a home back in Vegas to reside. All the wealth, fame, and fortune couldn't fill the void of having his family living in his beautiful estate with him and enjoying his bountiful harvest. He began thinking about hanging his jersey in the rafters beside Lamont and James. He thought about it often when he realized he'd already accomplished his goals. His entrepreneurial business skills had created him massive wealth with his real estate properties all over Las Vegas. So, the thought of retirement became his focal point. Rico felt his journey as Jackhammer Slim had abruptly come to end, but before he could even make such a decision, he had a flight to catch.

The United Kingdom

The eleven-hour and fifteen-minute flight from Las Vegas went smoothly. After watching a few movies and catching up on some well-needed rest, his plane landed safely at The London City airport. It was a rainy and cloudy afternoon, but the air smelled refreshing. Rico took in several deep breaths as he looked around admiring the amazing agriculture. London was interesting, but this wasn't his first time visiting. He'd been to London more times than he could count, but only to perform as The World-Famous Jackhammer Slim. Then, it was on to the next city. This time, he was going to make sure he enjoyed himself. He wanted to take this trip all in. Instead of calling for his usual Maybach luxury Mercedes to pick him up from the airport, he decided to take a ride on London's famous double-decker, two-story bus. After swiping his oyster cashless card, he walked straight to the top and began looking around admiring the scenery as a visiting tourist for the very first time. He wanted to take the breathtaking scenery of London all in before he arrived at the Kensington Estates in West London where James lived. It had been some time since he had caught up with James and he had a lot to fill him in on and he wanted to hear his thoughts on retirement.

Pulling up to the estate was epic. Rico knew James was a wealthy man, but damn. He was really living the good life. Upon entering his massive property, he was welcomed by a large steel gate and two enormously huge black armed security officers. Once he was identified and cleared, the drive to the estate was two hundred yards. The landscaping upon entering was staggering. James had everything you could imagine such as bronze statues, expensive-looking water fixtures, exotic plants, luxury masonry stonework, and more. He exited his Uber, looking around and shaking his head in awe. This estate made his mansion back in Vegas look like a bungalow. He began walking past James' fleet of Lamborghini's, Maybach's, and a breathtaking Rolls-Royce truck he hadn't seen in the United States. He took a couple of pictures and sent them to his assistant instructing him to find him one as soon as possible. Within a matter of seconds, the ten-foot wooden fiberglass door opened, and a familiar older man appeared. It was none other than Mr. Ellison.

"Big fella!" Rico said excitedly because he was happy to see him as the two embraced.

Mr. Ellison was James's security detail when he worked the Caesars Palace residency. The two bonded so well that James took him along with him when he retired.

"Rico, it's so good to see you again," he said smiling. "How are the kids?"

"They are getting bigger by the day. Aja just turned thirteen and Onyx is a sixteen-year-old, 6'3, 300-pound giant."

"My goodness! Father time awaits no man," Mr. Ellison replied.

"He sure don't!" Rico added as he entered the estate.

"James and Lamont are both in the back watching the Saints play. If you were anyone else besides the Merciful Allah, I would have told you he was busy. You know how much he loves his New Orleans Saints."

"Who you telling?" Rico replied laughing as he began walking towards the back of the massive estate.

The closer he got, the louder he heard clapping and cheering coming from no one other than the big homie, James himself. Rico made his way into the Great Room.

James looked up, and greeted, "Cheerio Mate!" He said it in the worst British accent ever, welcoming him.

He and Lamont were both relaxing in two of the biggest leather La-Z-Boys he'd ever seen and watching the football game on his 98-inch Samsung flat screen television.

"You had to have these custom-made," Rico said as he started admiring the leather recliners. "If not, I'm going to purchase two of these as soon as I get back home. I'm already getting that Royal's Royce truck you have parked out front!" he said laughing.

"You already know!" James replied. "That truck isn't scheduled to hit the showroom floor until next year, but I know the chairman, Roger Stovich, down at Royals Royce. I can give him a call and have him take good care of you. As far as the recliners, yes they are custom-made and one of a kind mate... but I can do you one, and have a couple of them shipped to your front door...on me, of course."

"What's the catch?" Rico asked knowing James.

"Something light! You just have to put on this New Orleans Saints hat and jersey, kickback, and enjoy the bloody game alongside me, Mate. So, what do you say?" James asked.

Rico laughed at his ridiculous accent. "That's all I have to do for two custom leather recliners?" he asked.

"Scout's honor, Mate," James said crossing his heart.

"Well, count me in then!"

James passed Rico a Saints ball cap and jersey. Lamont sat with his mouth wide open and shaking his head. He couldn't believe Rico fell for one of James over the top New Orleans Saints antics. He would do and give anything for some company, especially the type of company that cheered for his team.

Rico looked over at Lamont and said, "For two free custom-made leather recliners, it's on and popping. LET GO SAINTS!!" He yelled, while high-fiving James, as they continued watching the game.

The following morning, Rico was awakened by Mr. Ellison.

"Good morning, Rico. James sent me to tell you that breakfast starts in an hour." "That's cool. Thank you, Mr. Ellison." Rico replied getting out of the luxurious king-size bed.

He walked over to the sink and began washing his face and brushing his teeth. He started replaying over and over in his head what he wanted to say to Lamont and James. He wondered how they would react or feel about him wanting to retire. It wasn't like this was planned, but he felt this move was more than necessary.

The dining room table had to be at least twenty feet long. It had everything you could imagine you could eat for breakfast.

"Cheerio, Mates! Top of the morning, aye!" James greeted his entire table of friends and his 30-member staff of butlers and maids who lined the back wall looking confused as they listened to his awful British accent. Breaking the ice and causing the first laugh of the morning with his staff.

"Man, I must say, this is one hell of a pad!" Rico said.

"It's one of many," James replied. "I have another estate a little bigger than this one, yonder in Yorkshire.

"But why? Isn't this estate big enough?" Rico asked.

"Of course it is," James answered. "But why not when my harvest is plentiful."

"No doubt," Rico replied as he shook his head in agreement.

"So, what brings you all the way to London? I know you didn't come to see my estate or jack me for my automobile," James asked with a straight face and stern tone while stuffing his face with cheese eggs and turkey bacon.

"I've given this much thought, and I believed it was only respectful, that I told you face to face instead of over the phone."

"I appreciate that," James responded adjusting his Versace designer frames.

"Words could never explain how grateful I am that you gave me this opportunity. It's been an amazing journey full of unforgettable memories, and unbelievable wealth, but unfortunately, I think my time as Jackhammer Slim has come to an end. I'm ready to gracefully bow out and hang my Jersey in the rafters alongside yours and Uncle Lamont's... if you will allow me. My wife and kids need me in their lives more now than ever. Also, I would like to work more hands-on with my business ventures. I stay away on tour 250 days a year and trusting other people with my money and investments. I just think it's about time that I get my priorities in order and do what's best for me and my family.

"Understood," James said. "I never intended for you to be Jackhammer Slim for no longer than five years anyway. Don't forget your lifestyle was lived and experienced by me too. So, believe me when I say, I understand. The big question is, who's going to be your replacement? You do know that it is imperative, before you pass the torch, to make sure the next up-and-coming Jackhammer Slim knows how vital it is to protect our brand. Therefore, I'm holding you accountable and trusting in your decision to make sure that he practices and believes in the universal laws of attraction. Make sure that he realizes that it's not about validation or fame, but our brand. The women fantasize about Jackhammer Slim because he is a mystery. Destroy the mystery, you destroy the brand. Destroy the brand, you destroy the legacy. The future of Jackhammer Slim is going to be based solely on his mindset. Just as you can comfortably retire as a young black multimillionaire, so should the next Jackhammer Slim and the next after him. Since the unwritten law of becoming Jackhammer Slim is to never expose your identity, nobody knows how you look. So, not only can you retire, but you can retire and ride off into the sunset with peace of mind to enjoy your bountiful harvest because you did it the right way."

"Isn't that simply amazing?" Lamont interjected.

"No doubt!" Rico responded. "I never even thought about it that way."

"But we know you're with us," James replied.

Rico stood up and shook both their hands. James instructed his maids to fill their glasses with Dom Perignon Vintage 1951. "Let's all make a toast to Rico's amazing, Journey as Jackhammer Slim and to his well-deserved, bloody retirement... Cheerio!!"

Rico really enjoyed the sights and sounds of London, so he'd already made plans to visit again as soon as his retirement kicked in. James and Lamont were really living one hell of a life. He left London with a better understanding and respect for everything James and Lamont stood for and why. It was so imperative that he made the right decision in choosing the next Jackhammer Slim. With Lamont being the founder, James would eventually follow his amazing blueprint. By staying disciplined through the difficult challenges and testing of

the enemy, James stood ten toes on his beliefs.
Therefore, he was able to navigate his way through the
trials, tribulations, and overall chaos of life by being
surrounded by meditating and applying the universal
laws of attraction daily. Ultimately, this left him retired,
unscathed, and undeniably wealthy. Even to this day, he
continues to make millions, as long as Jackhammer Slim
tours and performs at the famous Ceasers Palace venue.

In retrospect, the next Jackhammer Slim will not only be
Rico's success story, but he will also secure the bag to
allow him to retire comfortably and create generational
wealth for himself and his family. He knew it wasn't
going to be a walk in the park, but he wouldn't have
wanted it any other way. He knew of the challenges that
were ahead and the work he was going to have to put
into finding him. Not to mention, it would all have to
happen while continuing to live out his personal goals
and aspirations of being a business mogul.

CHAPTER 2

The Main Event, Suffolk, VA

Rico continuously replayed in his mind what James told him back at his estate. He said the most amazing part about being Jackhammer Slim was the fact that he never really existed. Nobody knew of him or how he looked. He could walk anywhere on this planet as Rico, but if he were to put his mask on, in a matter of seconds, he could turn any establishment into an all-out frenzy. He knew the owner, Tee-Tee, because she was Lee-Lee's favorite niece. She took over three of her exotic club franchises after her long fight with breast cancer that, unfortunately, ended her life last year. Knowing how much her Aunt Lee-Lee loved them, she took a liking and embraced Rico, James, Lamont, and Vena as family. She kept in contact and developed her own personal relationship with each of them.

Rico entered The Main Event through the back entrance, greeted the bouncer, and walked straight to the back. There, he noticed several exotic dancers getting ready to perform. Some were listening to drill music and others were doing various workouts. Of course, the entire locker room reeked the smell of marijuana. The clouds were so thick he could barely see his way through. He noticed several liquor and beer bottles scattered throughout the chaotic locker room. He even spotted two men kissing and oiling each other's bodies.

"What the hell!" he said to himself as he was moving through the congested locker room as fast as he could. He was on a mission to find the next younger version of Jackhammer Slim, but it was evident that he wasn't going to be finding him at The Main Event. He knew he had to stay focused and positive because things were already starting to frustrate him.

The Colosseum At Caesars Palace

Jackhammer Slim was sitting in his dressing room after performing, yet another, sold-out venue when he was surprised by a fan who was able to sneak her way past his security. Luckily, he followed the blueprint, and he never took his mask off until he was back at his Caesars Palace residency. The woman stood there holding her composure. He sat in his chair looking back at her through his mirror. She had a familiar-looking shirt that read, I Love Me Some Jackhammer Slim.

"Can I help you?" he asked while picking up his phone and texting his security.

"I love me some Jackhammer!" she replied while pointing at her t-shirt. Suddenly, she began stripping naked. "Take me and have your way!!" she replied tossing her red silk Victoria's Secret boy shorts in his direction.

She stood seductively and had to be one of the most attractive women he'd seen in a while. Not to mention, her body was, without a doubt, amazing. Everything about her attracted him to her. He was turned all the way on, and it had been a while since he'd laid some serious pipe. Fortunately, within a matter of minutes, his security burst in and escorted the naked woman away. Rico locked his door and pulled his mask off. He was sweating bullets, which was weird because he never sweated like this on stage. He walked over to adjust the AC in his dressing room. That's when he noticed it was 70 degrees Celsius.

"That's strange," he thought to himself. "That woman was too beautiful to be a damn stalker," he thought. That's when he understood that she was just another test from the enemy, but he stood on business. Even though he knew, in his heart, that she was one of the most tempting ever, but the devil is a lie.

Another Day Another Dollar

The beautiful estate was located in the heart of Reno, Nevada. Rico arrived in his brand new burgundy 2025

Royals Royce truck. He stepped out sporting a red and black Ferragamo designer outfit, a Christian Louboutin leather cross-body bag, with a matching pair of Louboutin designer boots. He kept his accessories simple with just a plane Jane Rolex and a diamond pinky ring. He exited his vehicle and greeted his potential home buyers, a former judge, Anthony and his wife, Kim Harrison. They moved to Vegas from Florida and were looking for more of a paradise-at-home kind of feel with all the amenities of a vacation home. Luckily, Rico had the perfect estate for them.

"Good afternoon! Welcome to my open house."

Rico had purchased the estate for 800k as a foreclosure. He'd originally purchased it for Tamia and their children because he couldn't allow them to live at his current estate until he retired as Jackhammer Slim. His wife, Tamia, wasn't feeling that. Even though the estate was breathtaking and immaculate, Tamia declined it. So, he decided to sell it.

After investing almost 150k in renovations, he was looking to make a decent flip. He had five potential buyers stopping by for his open house who were all interested in placing their bid on the estate. By the end of the evening, he closed out at 2.2 million dollars.

The Devil Wears Red Bottoms

Rico arrived back to Caesars Palace around midnight. He exited his Luxury Maybach to a crowd of onlookers and, of course, the usual paparazzi were on the scene snapping pictures. Once they realized he didn't have security or an entourage, they thought him to be another wealthy tourist there to gamble. Suddenly, he noticed a familiar face walking towards him. It was Yancey Bazemore, a high school friend he kept in contact with from back in the day. She was now living in New York City as one of the top fashion designers at Fashion Solutions NYC. They had spoken on the phone months ago, but hadn't had the opportunity to meet due to both their hectic schedules. The last time she remembered seeing Rico, he was an exotic dancer. She and a couple of her girlfriends were leaving Caesars Palace's annual Balenciaga: RIP The Runway Fashion show, when she bumped into him.

Rico spotted her first. "Yancey Bazemore!!" he yelled.

"Rico Dallas! How are you? It's been a while. The last time I recall seeing you, you were dancing at that club in Virginia," she said looking up and trying to think of the name.

"The Main Event," he reminded her.

"Yes! That's correct!" she replied.

"But I'm doing well. Thank you for asking!" Rico said. "I see you looking beautiful. You look as if you picked up some good weight."

"Unintentionally, but I embrace the new me!" she said.

"Well, you look amazing."

"Thank you."

"I see you out here in Sin City. What you have going on?"
he asked.

"Working hard and still designing clothes. I just recently
launched my podcast, and it hit box office numbers. Over
two million viewers tuned in. I had Fabulous, ASAP
Rocky, and Lil' Jeremy featured as my first guest. They're
already labeling me the infamous Yancey Bazemore
because I spills the tea!"

"Congratulations! I'm proud of you," Rico said hugging
her.

"I'm just trying to leave my personal stamp on this radio
and fashion industry by any means. I see you're out in all
white tonight," she said looking him up and down.

"What are you wearing? Can I record the drip for my
fashion blog?" she asked while pulling out her iPhone.

"Of course!" he replied. "At least you asked." He was
referring to the paparazzi flashing their cameras without
his permission.

"Start from the top if you don't mind...and action," she
said.

"Okay, I love ball caps, so I copped the NY Yankee
leather adjustable. Got the white Cazal Soulja Boy hater

blocker frames on, ya digg? This here is the Allen
Cooper tailored leather motorcycle jacket, along with the
Balmain cocaine white polo shirt and custom joggers.
Shout out to my boy Dave Ross at Kick's Unlimited. He
hooked me up with these throwback, all-white, snake-
skin Air Force ones with the bubble gum soul. Ya digg!?
Accessories by my boy Keith down at Ice Tech
Diamonds. This here is the Rose gold Cuban link with
diamond baguettes and this special edition Audemars
Piguet wristwatch. My bracelet is rose gold flooded with
flawless baguettes.

"Yes!! I love that bracelet! It's glittering like a light show
on your wrist. It looks very expensive. What was the
ticket on it?"

"Sumthin' light!" he responded.

"I see you really been getting to that bag," she said.

"Just working hard so my children don't have to!" he
replied.

"I'm not going to hold you much longer. I know you're a
busy man. Thank you so much for your time." she said.

"It was my pleasure, and it was good seeing you again
too. We're going to have to link up soon. How long you
plan on being in Vegas?" he asked.

"Until tomorrow. My girls and I wanted to stay and watch Jackhammer Slim perform tonight. Since we're here, we might as well see a treat," she said giggling.

"So, you really like Jackhammer Slim like that?"

"Oh yeah! He just does something to me," she said shaking her shoulders as if she'd just caught the holy ghost or a cold breeze had just hit.

"I'm so jealous," Rico said laughing.

"No need to be!" she replied, walking away. "You're the real deal Ride Em' Rico Dallas! Jackhammer Slim is just a mystery. He really doesn't even exist," she said walking away.

That was confirmation to Rico's ears knowing he'd done his part in making sure the mystery of Jackhammer Slim remains anonymous. He made his way through Caesars Palace without a care in the world by walking pass hundreds of women and being social while interacting in various groups. He spotted multiple women wearing Jackhammer Slim apparel. Some were at the bar drinking, and others were gambling while waiting for his 10 o'clock show to begin.

None of them could have ever imagined that Jackhammer Slim himself was mingling amongst them all. He walked through a secluded entrance to get to a private elevator. The attendant recognized and greeted him right away. Then, he proceeded to press the button to the 29th-floor penthouse suite.

Uptown Norfolk, VA

Rico Dallas was born in Norfolk, VA. He was raised by his sister, Asia, after the sudden death of his mother, Gloria Dallas. She died of complications of the lungs when he was just 13. Doctors said her cancer was extensive due to her persistent cigarette smoking which caused her lungs to collapse. Rico was devastated, a mama's boy to the heart, he dealt with depression and mental health issues for years. His mother loved to sing, dance, and would play music in their home all day every day. Unfortunately, he never met his father. All he ever knew about him was that they called him Puerto Rican Juan and that he lived in the Bronx borough of New York City. He even hated when people called him Puerto Rican Rico. In his heart, he was as black as they come. Black as his favorite meal of hot dogs, pork and beans, drinking red Kool-Aid, while watching reruns of Sanford and Son and Good Times on television.

He knew nothing about his heritage and, yes, he blamed his father for it. He grew up claiming to be all black until puberty began to set in and the women began to fall in love with his hair texture and skin complexion. That's when he knew he was going to be a ladies' man. Years would pass and his newfound love for dancing came to fruition and he was booked to dance background for Usher Raymond on his World UR Experience tour,

22

featuring August Alsina and Cassidy. During this tour, he would get recognized as one of the best hip-hop dancers of his generation.

Opportunities and doors began to open for background dancers and Rico Dallas was at the top of the A- list every time. His big opportunity arrived when he received an unexpected call to report to Los Angeles, California in two days for a video shoot with a major recording artist. Unfortunately, the timing was bad because Tamia, his girlfriend at the time, was about to have their first child. He told his booking agent he couldn't make it. His booking agent swore to him that he was making a big mistake. Rico didn't care because he was determined to be there to watch his first son come into the world.

After fifteen hours of labor, Tamia gave birth to a healthy seven-pound eight-ounce baby boy, whom they named Onyx Marquell Dallas. Rico was proud to be a new dad and he wanted to be to Onyx what his father wasn't to him. He made a promise to his son, while holding him for the first time, that he would never leave him and would always love, cherish, and provide for him. Two weeks later, he called his booking agent and was informed that he'd been blacklisted from doing any gigs in the music and dance industry. From there he had no choice. He had a family to take care of by any means necessary, but doing anything illegal and risking going to jail was also out of the question.

The following day, he hooked up with a couple of friends, two local male strippers who were getting to the bag at the Main Event. Brian Perry, aka Blake Pumper, who was from Atlanta, GA by way of Norfolk, VA, and his younger cousin, Xavier Marshall, aka X-Man, who was from Chesapeake, Virginia. They told him they were both headed to Las Vegas to strip because they heard you could make up to five thousand a night. They suggested he should come and give it a try, at least for the weekend. If he didn't like it, he could be back on the first flight to Norfolk International.

With no steady income coming in and a newborn son to feed, Rico didn't hesitate to jump at the opportunity. He knew Tamia was going to have a big issue with it, but he was willing to put it all on the line. He had his mind made and he was determined that he was going to make it...no matter what.

CHAPTER 3

The Colosseum at Ceasers Palace was packed to capacity with women screaming at the top of their lungs over the music as Jackhammer Slim emerged from backstage holding a dozen red roses. He graced the stage with style and elegance as he began doing the crybaby and pumping away at the stage as if he were making love. Then, effortlessly, he would bounce back to his feet, slow grinding and winding to the sounds of Jodeci's, "Freak n' You." The closer he got to the end of the stage, the clearer his vision became. That's when he noticed a woman looking him dead in the face in the front row. It was none other than his friend, Yancey Bazemore. Alongside her were eight of her screaming friends. He noticed that something was different about her energy. She was the only person in the front row who wasn't screaming at the top of her lungs. Her arms were folded, and she was squinting her eyes to get a better look as if she knew something no one else did.

Boldly, Jackhammer walked over and passed her friend a rose first. Then, he made his way down and handed Yancey one, while watching her eyes the entire time. That's when he realized, what he knew for sure...she had noticed. He'd forgotten to take off his rose gold diamond bracelet that she loved so much.

Oh no he didn't...Yancey quietly thought to herself the entire drive back to their hotel. What a night! The bracelet that Jackhammer Slim was wearing looked too familiar. She couldn't wait to get back to her purse to retrieve her iPhone knowing for a fact she had a recording of it. Once there, she kept zooming in on Rico's wrist. Could this just be a coincidence or could Jackhammer Slim so happen to be the same height, build, and sport the same bracelet as Rico?

She began collectively gathering her thoughts and reminiscing back to their initial meeting just hours ago at the Caesars Palace casino. She thought about the Maybach he was chauffeured in and how his confident aura spoke volumes. Also, he used to be a stripper. In pursuit of being a fashion icon, she could eyeball any designer outfit and estimate the cost. She estimated, in total, that his outfit had to be around 10k and another 100k in jewelry at the least. She couldn't even recall if she asked Rico what he was doing in Las Vegas.

Who was he fooling? It was evident to her who Rico Dallas really was. She began thinking about the ratings, viewers, and just how much this information could skyrocket her podcast career to the top of the charts. She just had to prove it...

Caesars Palace Penthouse

Rico was back at his Vegas penthouse enraged, breaking bottles of champagne on the floor, punching holes in the walls, and screaming at the top of his lungs. He couldn't control his emotions.

How could I be so stupid? All the hard work and dedication I've put in the past five years meant nothing!!

One mistake was about to ruin his entire career and the Jackhammer Slim brand. He could hear James' voice in his head the entire time saying, "Destroy the mystery, you destroy the brand. Destroy the brand, you destroy the legacy." This was supposed to be his victory celebration. He was supposed to be riding off into the sunset retiring at 28 years old, kicking back while investing his money in real estate properties, and exploring business ventures across the country.

He lit several candles and began to meditate. In order to think his way through this situation, he knew he had to become one with the universe. After an hour of complete silence and breathing exercises, he felt better. His vision was a lot clearer and he instantly came up with a plan.

What's the use of having resources if you're not going to use them, Rico? he reminded himself while looking for his cell phone through the chaotic mess he'd just made.

He knew if anyone could help him, this person could, but his window of opportunity was getting shorter by the minute.

"Vena!? Hello!? Sis, how have you been? Do you know who this is?" he asked because he was surprised that she had answered. Vena stayed on the go, and normally one of several of her assistants would take her phone calls and messages.

"Your name did just pop up on my phone and you're the only person who calls me sis," she said laughing. "What's going on, Rico?"

"You have to promise to keep this between us."

"Okay!" she agreed thinking it was another relationship issue between him and his wife. Over the past five years, she had developed a close bond and mentored them both.

"I think we may have a whistleblower," he said.

"Oh, my goodness! How did you come to this conclusion?"

After several minutes of describing, in grave detail, his entire night, Vena also agreed that it was a strong possibility that Yancey would talk, especially being the radio personality and blogger she was. Vena advised Rico to calm down. She began saying that it was nothing new under the sun and that what was happening had already been done. Rico looked down at her on his iPhone with a confused look. She quickly recognized his frustration and informed him that the same thing had happened with James and Lee-Lee at The Main Event. "So, as I said, it's nothing new under the sun."

"Really!? Oh, now I understand where you're going with this. Damn, how did that happen?" he asked.

"Long story. We're just going to have to press the pedal to the metal to find the next Jackhammer Slim knowing the severity of the situation."

She informed Rico that she would be flying into the Harry Reid International Airport the following morning. He felt relieved knowing she had his back. Vena hung up and immediately called James to tell him exactly what she and Rico had just discussed. He wasn't even surprised. He understood knowing just how hard it was to be a public figure while trying not to be discovered. Rico didn't know it, but James was proud that he'd made it thus far.

Even though they've been up this road before, it wasn't going to be a walk in the park, but with the three of them putting their heads together, they could potentially come up with a plan to save the legacy of Jackhammer Slim.

"Isn't that ironic," Rico thought to himself looking at his phone vibrate. He'd hit the side button several times already. Yancey was blowing his phone to pieces. He knew he couldn't keep avoiding her or she would definitely get suspicious. He just needed a few days to get his thoughts together. He was scheduled to fly to Virginia for the weekend to spend time with his kids, but unfortunately, he had to let them know that something very important had come up. He did tell them that he would be there the following weekend though. Of course, they understood, but Tamia wasn't trying to hear it. She called him back minutes after he'd hung up with his children.

"Hello!?"

"I see you still putting them bitches before your kids again!!" she yelled into the phone.

"That's definitely not the case," Rico humbly replied knowing Tamia was just looking for any reason to argue. "I made plans myself to go out of town on business and wasn't expecting this at all."

"You're so fuckin' inconsiderate!" she yelled.

"Tamia, our kids are old enough to catch a flight to come visit me, but you won't allow that."

"Nope, and ain't! The way people are sex trafficking and kidnapping kids nowadays!"

"You sound stupid. Tamia, Onyx is a 6'3, 215-pound giant. Who's going to kidnap him?" he said laughing.

"That's your problem. You always think shit is funny. Don't show up tomorrow and see how long I laugh before you see them again!" she yelled before hanging up in his ear.

Tamia and Rico had known each other since middle school. He was the love of her life. They had been together for more than 10 years and were married for the five he stayed away. Rico decided to leave her and his child to pursue his dreams of becoming a famous dancer. She never knew exactly what he did in Vegas. All she knew was he danced background for a couple entertainers, and that he sold real estate properties as a side hustle. You couldn't have paid her a million dollars to believe he was The World-Famous Jackhammer Slim, but her woman's intuition would always tell her that he was hiding something. She felt as if she couldn't trust him anymore. Rico would fly home once a week with a bag full of cash. He kept it moderate. A light 10k didn't look too suspicious, but Tamia would still deny him sex often. She couldn't shake the feeling that she felt of being treated like another one of his whores he could just throw money at.

"You just can't make this shit up," is what he would often say to himself while sleeping on her living room couch knowing the opportunity he passed up on a nightly basis. However, since he knew he hadn't been keeping, it all the way one hundred with her, he took it all to the chin. That's why it was imperative that he hurried to find the next Jackhammer Slim. That way, he could one day sit her down and reveal to her the stranger he'd become the last five years of their marriage and the reason it was so important that he didn't tell a soul. He just prayed it wasn't too late.

Sometimes, he really wanted to say fuck it, but he loved his kids. Vena was scheduled to land in the morning, but his penthouse was, in no form, ready for her arrival. Rico stood in the middle of his penthouse confused and frustrated at the same time. While in disbelief and disgusted with himself, he looked around at the big mess he had made. He called his maids, Jessica and Reba, and asked them to come up and clean his penthouse. He wrote a note apologizing and left them both a two-thousand-dollar tip for the headache, while he went downstairs to play poker...

Manhattan New York, New York

Back at her office, Yancey had been surfing YouTube and looking at previous shows that Jackhammer Slim had performed. She looked for familiar traits that reminded her of Rico. Most of the videos were dark and the lighting sucked, but there was this one video where she could see clearly. With the help of artificial intelligence, she zoomed in and used facial recognition technology. She knew Rico Dallas had light hazel eyes. And with the help of A.I. This was going to be her moment of truth. The computer finished generating and it turned out that Jackhammer Slim had natural brown eyes. Yancey didn't know it for sure, but she was on the right track...just with the wrong person. What she just witnessed was a performance by the original Jackhammer Slim, James

Saunders, almost six years ago. Somehow, she was still determined to figure it out.

Harry Reid International Airport in Las Vegas, NV

Vena landed around noon at the Harry Reid International Airport in Las Vegas, NV. Landing strip twenty-one was cleared for her private jetliner. There, Rico stood beside his Maybach awaiting her arrival. As always, Vena exited the jet dressed in the best. She sported her long silky braid look under her Valentino Garavani hat. She was dressed in denim jeans, sporting channel designer frames, a Moncler leather jacket, and a leather pair of six-inch red bottom thigh highs. Her high-end style and grace demanded attention as she made her way down the steps.

Shaking her head and laughing at the silly look on Rico's face, she said, "No need to look pitiful. I'm here now! We have work to do. Time is money and we have to find the next Jackhammer Slim," she said as she entered his luxury Maybach.

CHAPTER 4

Tamia and her best friend, Tasha, had planned on spending their weekend girl's trip in the Dominican Republic. They both decide a vacation here in the States would be better due to the ongoing war in Israel and Gaza. They agreed that Las Vegas was the perfect destination. Tamia figured it would also be a good idea to stop by and pay Rico a visit. She thought about him the entire flight. She even talked Tasha's head off about how well he'd been treating her and the children and how she was thinking about being more open in allowing their children to fly to Vegas to visit him. After seeing a lot of teenagers on the plane alone and discussing it with the flight attendant, she realized that it was safe. She witnessed the flight attendants keeping their eyes on the children and checking to see if they were fine the entire flight. Even after the flight landed, they chaperoned each one to their expected guardian or Uber. The flight attendant said it would cost just a little more than a first-class ticket, but who puts a value on safety and the peace of mind of knowing your children made it to their destination safely? She also thought to herself that, just maybe, depending on how good he was looking tonight, she may just give him some.

"Make sure he calls a friend, for your friend. Okay!?" Tamia agreed while giving Tasha the side-eye knowing good and well she had a man back home in Norfolk.

"Girl, you already know. What happens in Vegas, stays in Vegas!!" they said in unison and laughing loud because they were drunker than Coolie Brown.

They partied and continued taking shots of tequila salt and lime shots their entire flight. Instead of calling Rico, Tamia decided she would drop by and surprise him. She gave the Uber driver his street address. Within fifteen minutes, they had arrived at one of the most elegant and breathtaking estates on that street.

"It's no way he lives here," Tamia said in awe of what she was witnessing.

She spotted several luxury automobiles parked in the driveway. She figured she had to be at the wrong house because, to her knowledge, Rico had nowhere near this amount of wealth. Right before she was about to advise her Uber driver to take them to their hotel, she spotted, what looked to be, Rico and another woman leaving the estate. Without hesitation, she called his phone and watched as he reached into his back pocket to retrieve it.

As soon as he answered, she hung up. "He didn't even have the audacity to call me back, "she said upset.

Minutes later, the luxury Maybach he and the woman who entered drove past them on their way out. At that very moment, words couldn't explain how hurt and humiliated she felt in front of her best friend. All she could do was lay her head on her shoulders and cry, but the friend in her wasn't going to allow Rico to spoil this girl's trip. She encouraged Tamia to put her big girl panties on, because they were in Vegas to have the time of their lives.

Navigate Your Way Through It

Yancey arrived at The Main Event around midnight. The club was packed to capacity. It had been years since she had been there. She looked around and so much had changed. It seemed so much bigger back then. Now, it just felt and smelled like a sweatbox. She began walking around the establishment with her four assistants and six of her best friends as they were dancing, buying drinks, and asking questions about Ride Em' Rico. She even had her assistant look up Jackhammer Slim's net worth, which was a whopping $150 million. That was a game-changer. She wasn't even focused on her podcast ratings anymore. This exposure had just turned into an all-out blackmail.

Yancey and her friends exited the establishment just as fast as they arrived, Then, they pulled out of the parking lot in a six-car motorcade. Their destination was Norfolk International Airport.

As soon as they left, Tee-Tee called Vena and told her what had just occurred.

"Thank you. We're on it!" Vena replied.

After she hung up, she looked over at Rico and said, "It's looking like Miss Thang is on a mission to pop your cherry, homie. That was Tee-Tee. She said Yancey was just at The Main Event asking questions about you and your whereabouts. She said the majority of the dancers didn't have a clue who you were and the ones who did said they hadn't seen you in years and they couldn't tell her what club you're currently performing at."

"This is starting to get ridiculous!" he said in a frustrating tone.

"It's going to be alright!" Vena assured. "I don't care how smart she thinks she is, she can't out-think us. What do James always say?" She asked, looking over at him. "It's the ones who can think their way through the chaos that's going to make it in this world. The chaos will always exist. The goal is to avoid being a part of it. You just have to think and navigate your way through it," she said with a confident and infectious smile.

He knew she was right because James had that effect on everyone in his circle. Vena's aura and energy was amazing. The both of them sat and listened to the smooth jazz sounds of Samara Joy as they drove off and into the beautiful Nevada sunset.

The following morning, Rico received an unexpected, yet uncharacteristic, call from Tamia. She sounded highly intoxicated and was all the way turned up! He looked at his Rolex and noticed it was barely five in the morning.

"Calm down! What's wrong?" he asked.

She hadn't had an ounce of rest and had been drinking and partying since last night. "Don't tell me to fuckin' calm down! I'm taking your black ass to court and you are going to sign away your parental rights. You're a cheating no good ass nigga, Rico! I knew it. I've always felt that you were a cheater. You could have just told me and let me live my life. Instead, you want to make broken promises and drag me along in your misery. I was a good woman to you. I take care of your kids! You a selfish bastard! I hate you!" she screamed in his ear.

He could also hear a voice in the background saying, "Girl, you don't need him. You're way too beautiful. You can have any man you want, and he will appreciate you. Hang up on his bum ass!"

"I'll see you in court cheater!" she yelled as she hung up.

At that very moment, he wanted to explode in a heap of rage, but he thought about everything he and Vena discussed the entire ride about him being able to think his way through the chaos. By far, this wasn't an easy task, and whoever the woman in the background was, didn't make matters better. With friends like her, who needs enemies? It all just seemed as if his house of cards were rapidly falling, but he knew he wasn't anything Tamia assumed. For Christ's sake, he was The World-Famous Jackhammer Slim, but he loved Tamia too much to cheat on her no matter what she thought. For the time being, he was willing to take it to the chin until he could prove to her his undeniable loyalty. So much was just happening at one time, but he understood how the enemy worked whenever he was out to destroy you. He comes ready to kill, steal, and destroy.

"The enemy knows, I'm about to ride off into the sunset, and into a bountiful harvest. I just have to stay positive," he reminded himself. "This too shall pass!" he thought while standing on his balcony and overlooking the beautiful courtyard at his multi-million-dollar estate.

Guess Who's Back...

Yancey and her team arrived at The Harry Reid International Airport around noon. She had planned on attending the Jackhammer Slim live performance later. So, she had her assistant call and request for nine V.I.P. front-row seats and meet-and-greet backstage passes. She was determined to discover the mystery of who Jackhammer Slim really was. She made this a personal mission to prove he was, none other than who she knew him to be, Rico Dallas from Norfolk, Virginia...

Rico was backstage trying his best to get his tangled web of thoughts in order. How was it even possible that he could get on the big stage and become The World-Famous Jackhammer Slim when his mind was all over the place? He knew the legacy of Jackhammer Slim still remained in his hands for now. So, it was imperative that he went out and gave the sellout crowd of 4,100 the best performance he could possibly give.

Regardless of how he felt, the show must go on. He could hear James in his head saying, "Greatness is earned, not given." He looked at himself in the mirror and said, "I'm very proud of you. It really takes a strong mental to go out and do what you do on a nightly basis, despite everything that's going on around you. You're the greatest Entertainer in the world. It's time to go and give the people, what they came to see!" With his own encouragement, he put his mask on and headed out onto the big stage.

Tamia and Tasha were both getting ready to attend the first show of his two live performances. Tasha couldn't wait to turn up.

"I'm getting freaky with somebody's husband, brother, son, uncle, nephew, or granddaddy tonight bitch!" she said laughing while taking another shot of Jose Cuervo, and Grey Goose. "Cause I know Jackhammer going to have something throbbing in these Victoria's Secret. It's time to turn all the way up."

"I agree!" Tamia said knowing she was going against her morals and values as a devoted wife and a Christian. She quickly dismissed the thought by taking another shot.

X-Man

Three hundred and sixty miles outside of Las Vegas, just off of exit mile marker 12 in Reno, Nevada, Vena sat at Flamingo's, one of the hottest male exotic clubs in the city. There, she noticed a couple of familiar faces and prospects entertaining the small crowd of women. One of those dancers was Xavier Marshall, aka X-Man. He was a part of her all-male review tour that she and James orchestrated for their exotic male dancing company, Second Chance Inc. He was known for choreographing several Missy Elliott videos and he toured the world dancing background for some of the biggest superstars in the business.

Vena recalled James loving the way he carried himself as an exotic dancer because he showed grace and professionalism. He also had amazing energy. Vena sat with him for more than two hours and not once did he smoke, drink, or talk disrespectfully in any way, shape, form, or fashion. He handled himself like a pure gentleman. He was respectful in the rarest form. She left feeling confident in him potentially becoming the next Jackhammer Slim, but she knew the last decision was supposed to be Rico's. From what Xavier discussed with her, the two of them had a falling out right before Lamont's injury so she knew it wouldn't go over well.

Vena had interviewed several other dancers, but none stood out to her the way Xavier had. He was her top pick of the litter. So, she decided to call and discuss it over the phone with James and Lamont. They all agreed due to this being an emergency situation.

The contract read:

> Xavier X-Man Marshall would begin acting as a temporary stand-in for Jackhammer Slim. It is required that a non-disclosure agreement is signed with the understanding that the sources of who Jackhammer Slim is will NEVER be revealed.

The stipulations of his contract stated that the term was for a total of 30 days and for the sum of $100,000. The contract also included instructions that he was to report to their choreographer immediately. He gladly accepted the opportunity and thanked Vena.

Meanwhile, the crowd of women were all screaming as The World-Famous Jackhammer Slim emerged from backstage winding and grinding on the stage. He looked into the crowd and there she was sitting front row and locked into his every move. It was none other than the infamous Yancey Bazemore and her group of friends he seen her with at his last show. Rico decided to take himself out of her clear view and head towards the end of the stage. It was there that he recognized a very familiar face. It was no one other than the love of his life, his wife, Tamia.

He laughed thinking to himself that he should call her up on the stage just for the hell of it. So, he pointed in her direction and had his security escort her to him thinking she would decline, but to his surprise, she damn near ran up onto the stage. Might as well make more memories he thought to himself still shocked that she was even there. He hugged her the second she entered his presence, and he passed her a rose while kissing her hand in the process. He also had his assistant bring forth his famous velvet red chair. This was going to be the most fun he ever had because he knew all the things that turned his woman on and he really wanted to see just how far she was willing to go.

Rico was having the time of his life seducing Tamia live on stage as she allowed him to caress her body in only a way her man should. As she sat with her eyes closed and enjoyed every sensual touch and his cologne. She told him that he smelled amazing. With 50 Cent's, "Candy Shop," playing in the background the crowd began going insane because he had never went in so hard on anyone the way he did with Tamia.

This was definitely going to make the Vegas Daily Press for sure. The women in the crowd began tossing their panties and bras while screaming at the top of their lungs with anticipation all wishing they could be the next lucky lady to experience his touch.

Tamia and Tasha left Caesars Palace around three in the morning. Tamia couldn't believe she allowed a complete stranger to caress her breast and grope her the way he had. It was almost as if he knew what she liked. His touch felt so familiar. He even nibbled on her ear lobe. Maybe, that was another reason she allowed him to do whatever he wanted. She felt comfortable in a weird way. She didn't even regret anything. She actually enjoyed every minute of his performance. She decided she was going to allow her inner bad girl to roam free with no regrets. Now, it was really time to turn up because what happens in Vegas, stays in Vegas.

Meanwhile, Yancey Bazemore and her crew were highly disappointed that he didn't choose one of them to bring onto the stage. After all, they were the baddest bitches in the building. Yancey's intuition was telling her that he was intentionally avoiding her, but he couldn't duck her for too much longer. She and her crew had all access meet-and-greet backstage passes. It was there where she planned on giving him his ultimatum.

CHAPTER 5

S traight Like That......

Yancey couldn't wait until her turn. She stood in line impatiently waiting for her opportunity to meet the mystery man she knew as Rico. She stood beside him and posed for the picture. Then, she whispered softly in his ear, "I know you're Rico hiding behind that mask. I'm going to need your filthy rich ass to wire five million dollars to my offshore account in Belize and I will keep my mouth shut. That's pennies to you and I know your identity means more to you than some money. If not, I'm going to reveal exactly who you are to my two million viewers next Friday night. You have my number. Talk to you soon," she said walking away.

He stood there emotionless like whatever she said, didn't even affect him, but it actually did. Luckily, he had his mask on because he really gave her the super sour, bitch face, but growth is amazing. He knew he could have easily made a phone call and offered ten thousand to have her dead by sunrise. However, he didn't want that karma. He knew how plentiful his harvest was about to be and he wasn't going to allow Yancey to mess it up for him. So, he quickly dismissed the thought. He knew the more positive he began to think, the harder the enemy was going to work to attack and distract him in all ways. Knowing this was all temporary and this too shall pass, he stood solid.

With everything going on in his life, Rico still found the time to manage his company. His real estate properties were selling, and he'd just purchased another mansion right outside of Vegas for a light million. With the added renovations, he was projected to make a three-million-dollar profit. He began learning the tricks of the trade and had made his decision. After retirement, he would go into full agent mode and start flipping and renovating properties while making millions of dollars and reinvesting it back into real estate. This would allow his money to make money for him and set up his personal goal of financial freedom and generational wealth for his children. So, he was not at all worried about Yancey's ass.

What Happens In Sin City, Stays In Sin City

Tamia and Tasha was downstairs in the casino playing Black Jack when two younger men walked up and introduced themselves as Flip and Santana Red. They said they were from California and were in Vegas looking for something to get into. They were very direct and Tamia liked that about them. She felt too grown to be playing games.

"How old are the both of you?" she asked.

"I'm 26, Flip replied, "and my boy Santana Red, he's 27."

She knew he boosted their ages, so she figured they were 23 and 22. She glanced over at Tasha for her approval, and she gave her the drunk nod.

"I mean, can a woman have a drink?" she asked.

"Hell yeah! My bad sexy lady," he replied. "I didn't want to offend you by asking. I just didn't see you drinking."

He was correct. She wasn't drinking because she was already drunk. This was actually her first time drinking this much in her entire adult life. After several cocktails and a whole lot of bumping and grinding on the dance floor, the ladies felt as if they were drunk enough to allow the young men to have their way with them. They needed an excuse in the morning for what they were about to participate in.

Collectively, they all decided to take the party up to their room. Tamia was so drunk she could barely walk. She had to take her heels off because she kept twisting her ankle and falling. Tamia wanted to be drunk to the point where she wouldn't remember a thing and Tasha was already there. The two men were having the time of their lives just having their way with the two drunk women. They even switched a couple of times.

By the end of their all-out sexcapade orgy, the two men decided to leave the two ladies asleep stretched out naked, but they weren't leaving without taking anything of value. Unfortunately, Tasha wasn't as drunk as they thought. She caught the thieves rummaging through both their purses looking for money and valuables. She stood her ground in trying her best to fight off the two men. Her constant screaming awakened Tamia out of her deep incoherent coma. She could only watch as she witnessed her friend Tasha kicking and screaming while getting strangled by Santana Red and fighting for her life. She could even recall hotel security kicking down the door and arresting them both, but unfortunately, it was too late.

The autopsy report stated that Tasha Unique Rodgers suffered blunt force contusions to the head. The report also read that mechanical force was applied externally to the neck causing strangulation, which caused her homicide.

Rico was just leaving Caesars Palace when he noticed that police and paramedics were all over the place. His assistant advised him that he heard that two women were just robbed and sexually assaulted and one of them was even killed. He said the perpetrators didn't even get far before they were finally caught and arrested.

"That's sad to hear," Rico said entering his Maybach. "People can't even have a nice time nowadays. I miss the late nineties," he said looking out of his window as they drove away from the chaotic scene on his way to have a long-awaited conversation with an old associate.

Tamia was rushed to the hospital where she was diagnosed with alcohol poisoning and was administered a rape kit. After her interview with detectives, they asked if she had anyone she could call to pick her up. She gave them her mother and father's number back in Chesapeake, VA. She was too embarrassed and ashamed to call Rico, who was just minutes away from the Sunrise Hospital and Medical Center where she was currently being treated. It was unfortunate that Tasha had to lose her life. Tamia knew that it was only by Allah's grace and mercy that she was still alive. To make matters worse, her nightmare was just beginning because she was now the prosecutor's star witness to her friend's murder. Now, she would have to take the witness stand in this high-profile trial.

Man To Man, We Can Talk About It

The studio wasn't that big. In fact, it was the size of Rico's master bedroom. He hadn't been there in a while, but it brought back memories of when he first became Jackhammer Slim. He could recall being nervous is hell while getting prepared for his first show. He remembered the sound of the crowd going insane the moment he took center stage, and how they screamed at his every move. It was as if he could do nothing wrong while on the big stage. He smirked as he reminisced about the days that used to give him butterflies. Now, it was just a regular day on the job.

His daydream was interrupted by Xavier walking up drenched in sweat to greet him. "It's been awhile ," Rico said extending his hand.

"Over five years, I presume," Xavier replied shaking his hand.

"The last time we saw one another, we were in Charlotte performing at the coliseum."

"Correct."

"That was the last I'd heard from or seen you until now. I forgot who told me you started dancing at Caesars Palace and was also selling luxury real estate properties all over Vegas. Are you the person here to show me the choreography?" Xavier asked.

"Not really," Rico responded, "that would be my boy, Tony Cooper. He should be walking through the door in a few minutes." Rico said looking at his Rolex watch. "But while I'm here, let's just address the elephant in the room. We grown men and we've all made mistakes. I could never get past you putting a mickey in that woman's drink when we were in Philadelphia. I hated you for doing that for real."

Xavier burst out laughing, "Man, that was a tic-tac and your boy, Lamont, was in on the joke as well. I know you have his number. You can call and ask him. They were saying her breath was smelling like dumpster juice. I happened to have a pack in my pocket. I offered her a couple and she declined. That's when Lamont told me to put it in her drink. I swear on my mother, it was candy! I would never do that to anyone. I understand how you could have taken it seriously."

"I did. I was watching from afar and was happy to see her get up and walk away."

Rico was an energy reader and he felt that Xavier was being straightforward and totally honest.

"Now, I remember," Xavier said looking up as if he was trying to remember something, "You didn't say anything else to me the entire male review tour after Philly. It was because of that?"

"Yeah!" Rico replied shaking his head.

"Five whole years, man. Over a tic-tac, but I'm happy we were able to talk man-to-man and address it."

"Me too. Now, let's move on. You just signed a contract to become the next Jackhammer Slim. This lifestyle can get lonely. Even though you will have and will be able to afford all the luxuries life can throw you, it's still a lonely profession. Nobody, including your closest family members, can know that you have become The Famous

Jackhammer Slim. He is to always remain anonymous.
For a decade, his true identity has never been revealed
because he is never the same person. You were chosen
and given the opportunity to become a part of a secret
brotherhood of multi-millionaires who have already
paved the way for men like you and me."

"Oh shit! So, you telling me that Jackhammer Slim has
been different people?" Xavier asked surprised.

"Yes! Remember, Jackhammer Slim is not a person, he is
a brand. It's more about not seeking validation, but
focusing on the task at hand. The moment you take your
mask off or even allow someone to expose your identity,
your career and contract will be terminated. It's about
you having the discipline to stay Xavier Marshall while
having the fame and fortune of Jackhammer Slim. It's
definitely not going to be a walk in the park, but it can
and has been done. The women fantasize about
Jackhammer Slim because he is a mystery. Destroy the
mystery, you destroy the brand. Destroy the brand, you
destroy the legacy. You have the opportunity to ride off
into the sunset while enjoying your bountiful harvest.
The future of the next Jackhammer Slim will be based
solely on your mindset. Last but not least, continue
studying the Quran, the 48 laws of power, and the laws of
attraction."

He gifted Xavier with several books of universal
knowledge. He told him new levels bring new devils,
and the enemy is going to be coming in all ways, shapes,

and energies. "These are just a few tools that can help you get through it." Rico looked up and observed Toney Cooper entering the studio with his backup dancers.

He passed Xavier his card and began walking away. For some strange reason, Xavier felt as though, Rico had been or was Jackhammer Slim.

"Can I ask you a question?" Xavier asked.

Rico turned around. "What's something Jackhammer Slim would tell me if he were standing here right now?"

Rico smirked at his question while taking off his Cartier designer frames and said, "I guess he would tell you that it gets lonely at the top, but it's well worth it," he said exiting the studio.

Rico received a call in the middle of the night from his son Onyx. He sounded upset. "What's wrong son? He asked.

"My mother is in the hospital!" he replied.

"The hospital!?" Rico repeated. "What happened?"

"She was raped."

"Huh? Onyx are you telling me my wife just got raped? Where is she? What hospital is she located?" Rico asked while trying his best to keep calm.

"Let me ask my grandmother," Onyx said putting the phone down.

Rico began pacing back and forth on the penthouse floor. He knew Tamia was supposed to be going away on vacation to the Dominican Republic, but he had just seduced her on the stage. "Maybe she flew to the Dominican Republic afterward," he thought to himself. He texted his pilot and told him to be on standby because he had to be wherever she was to support his wife. He also began texting his assistant telling him to cancel his next two shows.

"You can't make this shit up," he to himself under his breath.

"Ay, Dad?"

"I'm here son!"

"Mom's at the Sunrise Hospital and Medical Center."

"In Vegas!?" Rico asked surprised.

"I believe so Dad. She didn't go to the Dominican Republic. As far as I know, she went to Las Vegas with her friend Tasha."

The Sunrise Hospital and Medical Center was literally two blocks away from Caesars Palace. Rico began walking as fast as he could and trying his best not to overthink the situation.

It's Never Enough, But I'm Grateful

This was the most money he'd ever had at once that belonged to him. Walking out of the One Credit Union with a little less than a hundred thousand in cash, Xavier felt as if

he'd just hit the Nevada State lottery. The first thing he thought about doing was taking his daughter, Aaliyah, on a back-to-school all-out shopping spree. He was helping her grandmother, Mrs. Shirley, raise her. Aaliyah's mother, unexpectedly, passed away from Covid-19 last year and he's been active in helping to raise her ever since. This was going to be her freshman year in high school and he wanted to make sure she kicked the door down in style. He also wanted to purchase her a nice late-model Honda Accord. Everything he ever visualized doing for Aaliyah, he was now doing it. She was a smart and obedient kid, so he felt she deserved it. By the end of their full-day shopping spree, he'd spent fifteen thousand dollars. Five was spent on Aaliyah's wardrobe, hair, and nails. The other 10k was for her new Honda Accord. He also deposited 20k in her savings account.

These were just a few of the goals that he wanted to be able to accomplish. Just like that, he could only imagine what his future would hold. He could recall Rico saying to him, "This lifestyle can get lonely, even though you will be able to afford all of life's luxuries." He understood the assignment and the commitment he'd agreed upon, but if he could continue to put a smile on his daughter's face, then he was up for the challenge. For the next two weeks, he spent every day with Aaliyah, while pondering just how he was going to tell her that he was leaving, and wouldn't be coming back for a while.

Meanwhile, after a long investigation, Yancey couldn't find too much information on Rico. The Maybach he rode around in daily was in his name, and so were the several companies he ran. She slammed her laptop down in frustration from not being able to connect him to Jackhammer Slim. She looked down at her phone and decided she would give him another call just to see if he would answer. To her surprise he did.

"Hello?"

"So, you decided to finally pick up, huh?" Yancey asked in the softest tone.

"I've been busy as hell ripping and running. I sincerely apologize. This has been one of my busiest weeks. Even as we speak, I'm out of town in and out of business meetings." He was trying his best to distance himself as much as possible. "I just wanted to give you the courtesy of finally answering your call."

"Well, thank you, but did you think about my offer?"

"What offer?" he asked as if he had no idea what she was alluding to.

"The five million dollars," she replied.

"I don't think I have any properties going at that rate at this moment, but I do have a nice villa right outside of Vegas going for just under that and is scheduled to be available around next week."

"So, we playing dumb?"

"Look, I don't have a clue what you're referring to at this moment, but I'm returning back to Vegas next week. We can meet up and discuss further business negotiations then. Right now is not a good time."

"Sounds good to me," she agreed.

Rico hung up shaking his head trying to figure out just how he was going to shake Yancey off. She seemed determined to get that five million, which was nothing to him, but he knew if he paid her, it just would have led to more destruction, lies, and blackmail. Plus, the Jackhammer Slim brand was way bigger than her. He was just going to have to allow the universe to work through his thoughts. How could he, honestly, think about this right now when his mind is so clouded with everything going on? This nonsense wasn't even worth it at this moment when he didn't know what state his wife was in.

Rico entered the chaotic emergency room and approached the nurse's station. "I'm here to see Tamia Dallas."

The nurse typed her name in the computer. She looked back up at Rico and said, "Mrs. Dallas was discharged, literally, minutes ago."

"Do you know if she called an Uber or if anyone was here to pick her up?" He asked.

"No, I just remember giving her the discharge papers."

The Birth Of Yancey The Creator

Evette Yancey Bazemore, was born in Norfolk, VA to a single mother of three. With Evette being the eldest, she was expected to take care of her siblings while her mother worked two jobs to support them. Growing up sheltered, her childhood seemed unlikely, being that she was basically raising her two brothers. Seven days out of a week, she would immediately come home from school and begin cooking, cleaning, making sure they took their baths, and were in bed by 8 pm. At fourteen, that was a lot of responsibility, but she did it with no complaints. She loved her brothers, and she respected what her mother was doing to provide for them.

After her siblings were tucked in for the night, she would stand in the mirror and dance to her favorite songs. That was her "me time" because dancing and fashion was her therapy. Growing up Uptown, Evette was surrounded by the latest fashions. Her peers either had parents who spoiled them or they had boyfriends who hustled in the streets and would often give them money to get their hair and nails done and to go shopping. Unfortunately, her mother couldn't afford to buy her expensive clothes or give her money to get her hair done as often. She would give Evette a hundred dollars a month to do whatever she could do with it.

She never complained, in fact, she couldn't wait to get her hundred-dollar allowance. As soon as her mother paid her, she would immediately walk over to the Good Will thrift store. It was there she would allow her imagination to flow freely and would pretend she was shopping in a high-end storefront. She would begin picking clothing and certain fabrics she felt would look good and would go back home and sew them together. Often, coming up with her own creative styles, her outfits were one of a kind and she stuck out everywhere she went. People would always stop her and ask, where she'd purchase her outfits. That's when she knew she had a gift and could one day use it to get her family out of the poverty-stricken environment they were living in.

Her big break finally came when a local celebrity was picking her daughter up from the same school she attended. She noticed the outfit Evette was wearing and wanted to know where she had purchased it. Evette smiled and said she had designed it herself. The celebrity was blown away by her fashion sense. She loved it and asked if she could create an outfit for her. Evette agreed she would and the two exchanged information. Three weeks later, Evette was working on a custom design outfit for her client's up-and-coming shoot. She finished in time for the video. Just as expected, she nailed it.

The celebrity paid her three thousand for her outfit and gave her another two thousand as a bonus. Words couldn't explain how elated Evette was. She couldn't believe that someone would pay her for her designs. The celebrity's backup dancers entered into the studio to see the genius mind of this teenager. That's when she was introduced to them as Yancey The Creator by her celebrity client. She loved that name. For some reason, it represented the essence of who she was becoming, and ever since that day, she went by that name. She was even allowed the opportunity to live out her dream as a dancer when she was invited to go on tour and dance background for her. Her appetite for fashion grew stronger, and within a matter of weeks, she began designing for everyone in the industry.

Yancey The Creator was becoming a household name in the dance and fashion world. The contracts and money began pouring in at an alarming rate. At the age of fifteen and in a total of five months, she was able to purchase her mother a vehicle and move her family into a nice four-bedroom ranch-style home in Chesapeake, VA. She had already accomplished more than any of the privileged peers she grew up with. She started her own clothing line of t-shirts called, "Pretty Girls Have Big Foreheads," focusing on the insecurities that even pretty girls have while acknowledging the beautiful melanated skin they're in.

Yancey's Custom Designs grand opening was an instant success. Nobody believed this teenager would have taken the fashion world by storm at the rate she had. Pulling into the parking lot of her new business grand opening in style, Yancey gifted herself a brand new burgundy and black late-model Mercedes Benz. With over two hundred thousand in her bank account, she felt as if the world was her oyster. She began to get invites to celebrity parties and was introduced as Yancey The Creator. Everyone wanted the opportunity to work with her. She had so many appointments that she was booked for the next six months.

Dan Pulaski, a Jewish CEO of one of the biggest apparel companies on the East Coast, was looking for some newer talent to design clothing for him. After looking over Yancey's portfolio, he stamped her as one of the best he'd seen in years. He offered her two million dollars, a deal he'd never given out, but he wanted Yancey. So, he figured why not give her a deal she couldn't refuse, but to his surprise, she did!

Money didn't motivate her, and at that time in her life, she was still getting used to having it. She didn't like Dan's cocky approach, his aura, or his stuck-up personality. She couldn't even imagine working for someone like him. Respectfully, she declined his offer. She didn't want to make any commitments, especially being mindful of all the projects she had already committed to.

Unfortunately, that was the day her career in the fashion industry ended and she was blacked balled. She was labeled toxic and hard to work with. This shattered her dreams of becoming a fashion mogul. Later, she found out just how powerful Dan Pulaski was. She was informed that he'd sent out a memo and had threatened the entire fashion industry that if he heard she worked for any of them, he would no longer be doing business with their companies. Dan was a prideful man, and he was willing to end careers to prove it.

She would again try her best to climb the ladder of success by having a taste of fortune knowing she was right there. How could she allow one person ruin her life? She was determined never to give another man that much power again. Growing up in the Generation Z era, the internet became her tool for success. By all means, Yancey The Creator became a sensation overnight. She didn't grow up blessed to have laptops, iPhones, or even friends until she became Yancey.

Even though she didn't have as much money as she previously had, she looked the part every day. At the age of eighteen, her cousin, Erica, moved down from New York to VA. Unexpectedly, they bumped into one another at the local beauty salon. Erica looked happy, successful, and rich. She had on thousands in jewelry, and she also drove a newer model Tesla. Yancey couldn't help but to ask her what she was into. After going into grave detail about her hustle, without question, Yancey wanted in. So, Erica began teaching her how to scam people for money over the internet. She quickly learned the game and would, eventually, run her bag up to almost five hundred thousand by selling fake insurance policies.

After five months, she was caught, arrested, and sentenced to 20 months in federal prison. She was released early for good behavior, but unfortunately, she came home knowing that her mother was killed in an early morning accident. The police report stated that she fell asleep at the wheel, swerved off of the main road, and drove head-on into a light pole, killing her instantly. Her two brothers, Christopher and Donte, were both taken to CPS. Since she was a convicted felon, on probation, and without a stable home, she wasn't allowed to be granted custody. The house she purchased for her family had gotten infested with homeless crack fiends dwelling there. All she had left, was twenty thousand dollars, her name, and a big dream.

She hadn't been home for a month and had created a full two-hour length documentary. She shared intimate details of her rise and fall in the fashion industry such as how she turned down a two-million-dollar deal. She knew fans loved to hear a story of redemption. So, the following summer, The Rise And Fall Documentary of Yancey The Creator, was released and was an instant success. With over two million downloads and streams, along with another dancing gig with a major pop star, she felt as if she was back on the road to success. That was until she received a letter from the federal government stating that they were going to garnish all of her wages until the remaining balance of three hundred thousand dollars in court fees and fines were paid in full.

She quickly drove to the bank to withdraw her funds. She was later told by the clerk that her account had a federal freeze. She felt like she couldn't win for nothing. She needed to think and she needed a vacation. She called her girlfriends and they all decided to take a trip to Las Vegas to attend the Balenciaga fashion show. There she could shoot her shot with new designers, and try working her way back into the industry, or maybe even try dancing as a Vegas showgirl. She heard some of them were making six figures. She knew something had to give because money was rapidly going out and nothing was coming in. Just maybe she thought, she could find her golden opportunity there in Sin City.

CHAPTER 6

Rico searched far and wide. Every bus stop and train station. He constantly called her phone, but it kept going to voicemail. Words couldn't explain how he felt. As her husband, he was supposed to be her protector, her security, and her anchor, yet he hadn't been either.

He found a park bench and sat down. He needed to relax and think his way through the chaos. He closed his eyes and took several deep breaths. He began focusing on happy thoughts. He started visualizing a big, beautiful ocean. Then, he thought about spending the holidays with family and friends. He visualized his children being happy and healthy. His wife being very excited to see him. Suddenly, he became one with the universe, by manifesting his own piece of mind. Then, to his surprise, he could think clearly again. He knew his wife like the back of his hand. Rico looked down at his Rolex and seen it was 10:30 on a Sunday morning. If his memory served him correctly, he knew exactly where his wife could be.

Tamia had her mother send her a thousand dollars from Western Union. She offered another customer a hundred dollars to drive her to the airport. She arrived fifteen minutes before the flight to Norfolk, VA was scheduled to depart. With only minutes left, she safely boarded and headed back home to her mother and children. She sat on the plane ashamed of the way she behaved. She kept playing back over, and over in her head, what she could have done differently. Just maybe, Tasha would still be alive. Her entire Vegas experience was a nightmare from the beginning. She wanted so badly to call her husband, but her pride wouldn't allow her, especially knowing how she'd just fussed and cursed him. She even threatened to keep the kids away, so why would he want to help her?

When Tamia found out that Onyx informed Rico about her being hospitalized, she began to think negative thoughts and turned the blame on everyone besides herself. "Hell, he didn't even bother to come and check to see if I was okay," she murmured under her breath as she thought about everything.

She wanted to shift the blame so badly on Rico, but she knew she was wrong.

Onyx called regularly and kept his father updated. He told him that his mother was on her way home and that her flight was scheduled to land around five-thirty. Rico was at a loss for words while trying to figure out what the hell was happening with Tamia.

Only the Beginning

Xavier was still making his rounds of due diligence. He wanted to make sure Mrs. Shirley was debt-free. He knew she received social security along with a retirement check each month. So, he figured he would pay her mortgage for the next six months. He thought it was only right because she was his daughter's caretaker. He also gifted her twenty thousand in cash. "The money isn't a payment," he told Mrs. Shirley when she didn't want to accept it, "It's just a token of my appreciation," he reminded her. Xavier just wanted to make the bills a little lighter on her. He also had to mentally prepare himself for the talk he was about to have with Aaliyah. He didn't know how well she was going to take him leaving to go to Vegas.

Xavier thought she wasn't going to take it well, but to his surprise, she did. Xavier hugged Aaliyah and told her to hold down the fort before leaving out of the door. His flight landed in Vegas around midnight. Xavier picked up his luggage and headed towards the front exit of the airport. There, he noticed a beautiful black Maybach fresh off the showroom floor. The chauffeur was holding a sign that read, Xavier Marshall. He nodded towards him acknowledging that was who he was looking for. The chauffeur introduced himself as Orlando and gently opened the door to allow him access.

Orlando said he'd been living in Vegas for 10 years, had four children, and was a very hard worker. Xavier felt as though his introduction was voluntary and a bit too open. So, he decided to remain silent while enjoying the ride and admiring the bright lights of Sin City. When he arrived at his destination, his chauffeur exited to open his door. He dismissed his courtesy and tipped him a hundred dollars.

"Thank you and have a blessed day!" he told Orlando, which left him with a confused look on his face.

The studio was packed and Toney Cooper was already preparing for his arrival. As soon as Xavier entered all he heard was, "Chop, Chop, let's get dressed. Time is money and neither one of us has time or a dollar to waste."

The dance session felt more like a workout session. Xavier felt beat down afterward. He looked up and in the far back corner, he spotted Rico. The two embraced as Rico welcomed him to Vegas.

"Thank you," Xavier replied.

"You did well. That choreography routine was fire. I forgot how good of a dancer you actually are. I'm impressed," Rico said proudly.

Xavier could do flips and handstands on one arm. Rico knew his youthful physical appearance was sure to please the women.

"How about you meet me at the sports bar tonight? We can talk more, there," Rico said. "But for the time being, here is your Caesars Palace room key."

"Damn! I thought I get the Penthouse suite," Xavier said laughing.

"It depends on how well you maintain throughout this probationary period," Rico replied as he walked away.

As the two of them exited, Xavier spotted the black Maybach still parked with the Spanish driver, Orlando, standing beside it reading a magazine. After he'd been in the studio for close to three hours.

"I'm definitely not paying that tab," he said pointing at the luxury vehicle. "I never told him to wait for me."

Rico was wondering what the hell Xavier talking about. "What tab? That vehicle belongs to you, and Orlando's your personal chauffeur," Rico said laughing.

"Stop playing!" Xavier replied.

 "I wouldn't play like that. Why do you think he hasn't gone anywhere yet? That's just one of many gifts from the brotherhood."

"Word?" Xavier responded in awe. "I'm going to have to pull up in this. I really don't like being chauffeured. Can I drive it myself?" he asked.

"It's totally up to you, but let me warn you, the way people drive out here is insane. Personally, I prefer an experienced driver who knows the demographics of the city, but it's your vehicle. You can do as you please," Rico entered his vehicle and drove away looking back at Xavier standing in awe and admiring his new million-dollar Maybach.

Rico had a good feeling about Xavier. He was different and he possessed the energy, vibe, and charisma needed to become the next Jackhammer Slim. Just as his journey was coming to an end, Xavier's was beginning. He personally knew the obstacles and challenges that were ahead, but he felt comfortable passing the torch. He began thinking about moving his family out to Las Vegas or maybe even out of the country for a few years. He reached down into his jacket to retrieve his phone. He called Onyx to get an update on his wife. To his surprise, Tamia answered.

His room at Caesars Palace was immaculate. Xavier looked around at the square footage and was amazed. If this was a regular-sized room, he could only imagine how big the

penthouse suite was. He thought to himself while sitting his luggage down. He wasn't there three minutes before there was a knock at the door. He answered, and there stood a giant towering above him. He introduced himself as Big Will and said that Rico hired him to be his security twenty-four hours a day, seven days a week.

"Damn, do you ever get any time off?" Xavier asked.

Will began laughing and replied, "That's totally up to you, boss!"

"Just call me Zae!" Xavier said.

"Okay Zae, would you like a tour of Sin City?

"Hell yeah!" Xavier replied. "Just let me grab a few things and my phone," they exited the room and entered a private elevator.

The doors opened to the basement. It was there where he noticed the valet parking service stood. They walked right past them because you couldn't miss it. Parked in a reserved parking space was his beautiful black-on-black Maybach S680. Big Will asked Xavier for his car keys.

"Oh no, I'm doing all the driving," he replied. "You can get your big, tall ass in the back and relax. I'm not tripping at all!" Xavier said while getting into the driver's seat.

For three hours straight, the two of them drove around Las Vegas, Nevada touring the beautiful scenery of Sin City.

"So, where are you from?" Xavier asked.

"I'm originally from the Northside of Moncreif in Jacksonville, Florida. I moved to Portsmouth a few years back got into some trouble and did a little stretch. When

I came home, my Uncle Ellison hired me to do security for his private firm and the rest is history."

"You look young as hell. How old are you? "

"I'm twenty-five," he replied.

"With your size, there's no way you couldn't have made it to the NBA," Xavier said while looking back at him through his rearview.

"Believe it or not, Zae, I've never been a fan of playing or even watching basketball. I'm a Florida boy. We like football and love baseball. How tall are you anyways?" Xavier asked.

"I'm 6'6, 300-pounds," he replied.

"Man, I'm nicknaming you Oak Tree from this point on," Xavier said.

"I'm cool with it," he replied laughing.

"I'm actually from VA myself. I've been dancing for over a decade. I've toured the world dancing background for several well-known celebrities…in hopes of making it big someday. Honestly, I was just a day away from quitting my night gig when Vena walked into the club and interviewed me right there on the spot. I couldn't have been happier to get the hell out of that sweatbox. I'm definitely going to make the best of this opportunity. I also have a beautiful daughter back home named

Aaliyah. This will be my first time being away from her. Damn, I miss her already just talking about it.”

Xavier pulled into the gas station packed with cars and people standing around. He and Big Will stepped out and looked up at The World-Famous Jackhammer Slim billboard.

“Is that you?” Big Will asked.

“You already know the count! I’m pretty sure Rico and Mr. Ellison already schooled you.”

“They did!” he said laughing. “I was just checking your temperature.”

Suddenly, people began walking up asking Oak Tree for autographs thinking he was a celebrity or played football for the Raiders. They looked at Xavier as his driver as he walked past the crowd effortlessly to get him a couple of snacks and looked back laughing because they had no clue.

Communication

“Tamia! How you doing baby?”

“I’m okay.”

He wanted so badly to ask her why she didn’t call for his help when he was just five minutes away, knowing she needed money, clothing, and shelter. He wanted to drill her with 21 questions, but what difference would it have made? All that mattered was that she was back home safely. He told her that he was sorry for what happened to her and that whenever she felt comfortable talking to not hesitate to call.

She thanked him and said that it was only by God's grace and mercy that she was still here. She also told him that the only reason she hadn't called was that she and her parents had been praying and fasting since she arrived back home. Tamia grew up in a Christian home. Her father was a devoted minister, and her mother was the First Lady at the New Rising Sun Baptist Church, where he was the pastor for more the 20 years.

He reminisced back when he'd gotten Tamia pregnant with their first child, Onyx. She had just turned 20 and he and his friends were shooting hoops when she approached him. She interrupted their game, reached into her purse, and pulled out a positive pregnancy test. Then said that they would have to get married or her parents would be devastated. They did get married, but for all the wrong reasons. Ever since, their relationship has gone through seasons of trials and tribulations in their journey of love, growth, and happiness.

Rico was taking baby steps toward improving his communication with Tamia. Even though he really didn't have the time, he was willing to make time just to have better communication with his wife. He knew, in life, that everything good and evil came with a sacrifice. In life, you will always have to give something up in order to receive. He knew it was just a matter of time before he would reveal his deepest secret to her along with their bountiful harvest.

Rico was back at Ceasers Palace talking with Vena, James, and Lamont via WhatsApp. Collectively, they came up with three different ways to shake off Yancey. It wasn't going to be a walk in the park, but it could be done. They also wanted to implement Xavier into their real estate and extended joint ventures to set him up to become a multi-millionaire for the remainder of his life. The Jackhammer Slim brand was expanding in businesses all over the United States. One by one, their members were hand-picked and indoctrinated into their secret brotherhood for life.

Celebrity Life

"Boss, I'm definitely not feeling this celebrity life," Big Will added. "I mean riding in the backseat of this Maybach every day is an amazing experience, but these star-struck people are starting to get on my last nerve!"

Xavier began laughing. "Damn Oak Tree, you not feeling the limelight huh?"

"Hell to the no!" he replied. "I do security for you. I never signed up to be a distraction for you," he said laughing.

"Okay, I got you. I'm going to drive down Sunset one last time and then she's all yours. I guess I'm going to sit my gas-happy ass down and enjoy the ride."

"That's right!" Big Will added while lying back and watching TV.

All A Misunderstanding

Tamia and Rico finally caught up with one another after a long five-month hiatus. She walked into his hotel room dressed in her red and black Dior sweatsuit and wearing matching Jordan 4's.

"You looking cute," Rico said when he answered the door.

The two embraced for what seemed to be seconds, but it was actually minutes. Tamia smelled wonderful as always.

"So, first of all, thank you for coming. I wanted to have an open conversation with you without judgment or pointing fingers. So, I'm going to start by saying, I apologize for my absence and not being there for you mentally, spiritually, as well as physically. You have been nothing but the best mother and wife to me and our children and I sincerely apologize."

"Rico, I appreciate you for that apology," she replied as she looked up towards Rico.

Rico noticed that her entire facial expression had changed. It was if she'd been waiting to hear that for a lifetime.

"It's so hard trying to figure your man out and raise a family at the same time. You get to the point where you just stop caring," she replied.

"I understand," he said, "in just a few weeks I will finally be able to explain everything. I know that's not what you came to hear, but trust me and believe that I'm just as ready to tell you as much as you want to know."

Tamia sat quietly listening shaking her head in confusion. "So, you telling me you are in a secret society?"

"Something like that," he replied.

"Some Illuminati shit, Rico? Oh lord! Please don't tell me you then went and sold your soul."

He burst out laughing. "Damn, I needed that laugh. It's definitely not the Illuminati, but more of a secret brotherhood. It's more positive than anything. I took an oath to not disclose anything until the appropriate time. Since you're my wife, I can reveal it to you and only you."

Tamia looked at Rico and said, "You better not be gay!"

"Far from it," he replied while shaking his head and laughing again.

"So, who was that rich woman you were riding with last Tuesday night?" Tamia asked.

"Last Tuesday…" he began thinking. "In Vegas?"

"Yes!" she said in a matter-of-fact tone while standing with her hands on her hips. "Dark-skinned, short, long braids...the both of you got into her Maybach and drove away.

The only person he could recall doing that with was Vena. At that very moment, everything began to make sense. He recalled him and Vena exiting the mansion. She took notice first of the strange vehicle parked along the street.

"I brushed it off as paparazzi, but when we drove past, I looked directly into the vehicle. I didn't get a good look, but I thought I recognized you.

"So, why didn't you stop?"

"Because I wasn't sure, but you knew it was me and you didn't stop the vehicle," he replied.

She got quiet as if she were there thinking. "So, you're saying that woman in the car with you was Mrs. Vena?"

"Scout's honor!" he said crossing his heart with his finger. "You never seen her, but you've talked to her on numerous occasions."

"She's beautiful," Tamia said.

"And so are you baby," he replied walking over to embrace his wife.

He began kissing and caressing her entire body touching her in places he knew turned her on. She began returning the jesters as if she knew where this was going. That's when he, effortlessly, picked her up from off of her feet and began walking towards his bedroom. It was definitely on and popping.

Know your Limits

The karaoke bar was lit! The energy was amazing, the service was good, the food was delicious, and the crowd was full of beautiful drunk women destroying the words to the songs that were being displayed across the screen. Everyone was having the time of their lives. Xavier noted to himself to visit this night spot again. After his first drink, he said he wouldn't have another, but after singing several songs back to back, he developed a dry throat. So, he requested for the waitress, Mya, to keep them coming. He even passed Will a couple of shots of Hennessy.

They knew their limits and Xavier knew he was close to his. Suddenly, three women walked over to their table and introduced themselves, as Veronica, Ebony, and Jessica. They said they were all from Texas and just visiting Sin City for the weekend. Xavier couldn't take his eyes off of this one chick. She was fine and thicker than a Webster Dictionary. Texas breed some thick women. He leaned over to tell it to Will. He adjusted to get a better look and strongly agreed. They invited the group of women to join them. Xavier called the waitress

back over and ordered rounds for everyone. He wanted
to enjoy his last weekend as a regular person. He knew
the mission that he signed up for. He also understood
the moment he became Jackhammer Slim, that his days
of drinking and partying would be over.

"Mya! Can we get another round, please?" he yelled over
the music.

Bait and Switch

Rico finally called to set up the meeting with Yancey.
How ironic was it that she set the time and date on the
debut of Jackhammer Slim performing live at the
Mercedes Benz Super Dome in New Orleans,
Louisiana.

"That's perfect!" Rico replied.

"You sure?" Yancey asked while giggling and being
facetious.

"Absolutely, that's perfect," he said with the biggest smirk
on his face knowing Xavier was going to be the one
showing up and showing out on that big stage.

He decided that he was going to fly her out in two days
to meet with him in the Dominican Republic. Xavier's
debut was in three days. He had several real estate
investments he was closing out on, and he thought it
would be cool to show her exactly what he did to make
his money.

Tamia was back home talking with her mother about their meeting. "It's almost as if he can't tell me anything until a certain day. I was so confused, Mom."

"I understand baby. Well, at least he told you he was going to reveal it to you when he arrived back from closing his real estate deals in a couple of days. Until then, I guess you're just going to have to wait it out!"

The seven-hour flight from Las Vegas to the Dominican Republic went smoothly. Rico and Yancey sat beside one another the entire flight just getting to know one another. Rico talked about how life was living in the mean streets of Norfolk, and Yancey, of course, could relate. They talked for hours. They even ate steak, baked potatoes, and drank champagne for the remainder of the flight. After hearing Yancey's life struggles, he understood why she was behaving so badly, but it still wasn't an excuse for blackmail.

Surprisingly, she still hasn't said anything about the money or made accusations that he was The World-Famous Jackhammer Slim. Arriving at the property, it was beautiful. The mansion sat on a three-acre lot, overlooking the beautiful island of Cayo Levantado. "This here is one of three properties I just purchased for a million dollars. After I do my renovations, I'm looking to receive around three million."

"That's a decent flip," Yancey said looking at the estate.

He took her to see two more just like it and said that he was also expecting millions back on the return. Yancey was actually starting to look at him differently until he received a call that changed his energy completely. Whatever it was, they told him to pull it up on his phone.

It read.....

> The toxicology report read that the driver was impaired and that his alcohol blood level was 1.5, way above the legal limit. The 2023 Mercedes Maybach he drove was said to have run the red light at the intersection of Brooklyn Park and Chamberlayne, crashing into two other vehicles including the driver of an SUV who died at the scene. Along with the driver of the Maybach, twenty-five-year-old Xavier Marshall from Chesapeake, Virginia.

Words couldn't explain the feeling that was stored in him at that very moment. His mind began to race, but there was no way he could get to New Orleans in three hours to perform. The flight was eight hours minimum. His entire life had just flashed in front of him. He felt defeated as if he'd disappointed his family, the brotherhood, and the legacy of the Jackhammer Slim brand. He was supposed to be there with Xavier every step of the way, but he was too busy trying to shake off Yancey. He immediately called Vena to deliver the bad news, but to his surprise, she had already heard. He thought they just needed to cancel the show and just pay Yancey the five million.

She said she was on it and for him to continue on with the plan. He hung up sad, confused, and distraught at the same time.

"Is everything okay?"

He reminded himself to stick to the script. "Not really Yancey. A close friend of mine just was killed in a bad accident.

"My condolences," she said. "We may need to wrap this up so you can get back home."

"It's no rush. Our flight doesn't leave until tomorrow evening. Let's get back to our Airbnb. I have a serious headache.

Yancey was studying his walk and compared it to the YouTube video of Jackhammer Slim that she was watching. She didn't want to make a fool out of herself, so she patiently waited for the concert to begin in two hours. She knew it was no way in the world he could be there and in the Dominican Republic with her at the same time.

Rico, on the other hand, was in a complete panic. He continued calling Vena's phone, but to no avail. He began to think she was going to call and advise him to pay Yancey the hush money because, at this point, if the concert was to get canceled, it was more than likely his cover would be blown. Rico took two Tylenol and went to sleep.

He was awakened by Yancey's loud conversation. He looked at his Rolex and noticed he hadn't been asleep a full hour. "What the hell is going on?"

He rose from out of his bed and quickly knocked on Yancey's door. She seemed really excited.

"What's all the hype about?" he asked.

My girlfriends went to the Jackhammer Slim show tonight and he pulled my friend Chrissy up onto the stage. My friend Kim is recording it live!!"

Rico stood looking at Yancey's phone in awe trying his best to figure out just who Jackhammer Slim was. He began feeling like the fans and he realized that the mystery alone was exciting, but this Jackhammer Slim dancer was official. He didn't want to look too much longer, but he felt amazing. It was like a breath of life had just been blown into his lungs. Once again, the brotherhood came up with another conscientious plan to overcome their opposition. He couldn't wait to get back to Las Vegas so he could WhatsApp the team to see just how that play went down.

Around eleven that night, Rico received a knock at his door. It was Yancey. She stood dressed in her red bottom Louis Vuitton stilettos with her breast exposed and wearing a pair of red Victoria's Secret boy shorts. She looked absolutely stunning. That prison sentence had done her some justice because she was stacked!

"Would you like some company?" she asked.

"Hell yeah!" was his initial thought because staring at Yancey busting through them boy shorts was a sight for sore eyes. She had pissed him off so bad, that he'd forgotten how sexy, thick, and curvaceous she actually was, but Rico knew she was all worked up from watching Jackhammer Slim perform the past hour. Unfortunately for her, he wouldn't be fulfilling her erotic desires tonight. He wasn't willing to betray the love and loyalty he shared with his wife Tamia. No matter how good Yancey looked, he knew she was just another distraction from the enemy. Not to mention, she did try to blackmail him the entire time. That was definitely a turnoff. Even though she looked inviting, he respectfully declined. He just wanted to be able to look his wife in her beautiful eyes knowing they shared a love and loyalty that could never be broken. No matter what they were going through or how long they were apart. So, he told Yancey he didn't feel comfortable with her dressed half-naked around him because he was a married man and he didn't want to disrespect his relationship. She rolled her eyes and walked away.

CHAPTER 7

Back In Las Vegas

After he departed ways with Yancey, Rico immediately called Vena. She answered and gave him the tea. "Turns out, Xavier and Will were both out on the town at a local karaoke bar. I talked to the waitress working that shift and she recalled Xavier entering the bar around eleven. She said he sat at the back table with a group of women for over an hour. They ordered food and shots of tequila. She said that Xavier personally requested that she keep the drinks coming throughout the night. She said that he tipped her five hundred dollars and left the club around midnight."

"How did you find out about his death?" Rico asked.

"Will called me from the scene of the accident," she replied. "He wasn't injured because, for some strange reason, they said that he was the passenger in the vehicle that Xavier was driving."

"Oh yeah, the day I gifted him the Maybach, he told me he didn't want a chauffeur. So, I'm guessing he drove and Will survived by riding in the back."

"Hold on," Vena said, "that's James and William calling now. I'm going to merge their calls."

"Hello, hello...James and Will, are you there?"

"Yes, we are."

" I have Rico on the line."

"It's very unfortunate that we lost our Xavier before he became an official member of the brotherhood," James said. "The lesson in this life experience is to always stay disciplined no matter what. It's a proven fact that if you follow the blueprint, you will receive a bountiful harvest. It's no shortcuts and you can't add on or take away. It's already written in stone. The question now is, where do we go from here? I'm really too old to be shaking this ding-a-ling on anybody's stage!"

They all burst out laughing. "How did you get to New Orleans in time?" Rico asked.

"I was in Norfolk visiting family when I received the call from Vena. She told me you were handling the situation with Yancey over in the DR. So, without hesitation, I jumped on my PJ and was there in two hours flat. I didn't have time to take a piss before they were calling for me to hit the main stage."

"You wasn't even ready," Rico added.

"I stay ready, so I don't need to get ready!" James replied. "Rico, we're each other's insurance policies. That's another reason why it is imperative that we continue to stay physically fit. Even after retirement, in the event something like this happens, preparation is always pivotal. The Caesars Palace venue is booked for the next three months. Unfortunately, you won't be hanging your jersey in the rafters anytime soon. It's going to take a lot of work to find the next Jackhammer Slim, but he is definitely out there. We will work diligently to make sure you get your retirement as soon as we can. Will is now assigned to protect you. He should be there by the end of the day correct, Will?"

"I'm on it boss," he replied.

"With that being said, stay positive and productive," James said before hanging up.

Vena and Will were both still on the phone.

"This shit is crazy! My entire life is on hold. I promised my ole lady so much! You just don't understand," he wailed.

"And I do Rico," Vena replied. "I can have a woman-to-woman sit down with Tamia next week, if you would like me to. I can discuss your job description without going into any details. Giving her a better understanding of this whole ordeal, so that she doesn't feel misled or like she's being lied to!"

"Please, Vena! I would appreciate that!" he replied.

"No problem," she said. "Also, I'm going to need Xavier's daughter's full name and social security number. As soon as I get back to our headquarters, I will have my secretary deposit some funds into her savings and I'm donating to her father's charity.

"That's so generous of you," Rico added.

"It's the gift that keeps on giving," she said before hanging up.

Rico was back to square one...so much for early retirement. He had more work to put in as The World-Famous Jackhammer Slim. He headed over to Ceasers Palace where he sat back and recollected the events that occurred this week. You just can't make this shit up, he thought.

His entire schedule was booked from now until the end of the month. He took a deep breath and reminded himself to embrace the journey. He knew that everything he was going through was only temporary and it too shall pass. He had to get some well-needed rest. It had been a long and challenging week. Plus, Tania's preliminary hearing was at 9 am.

Tamia was at her layover in Texas. Her flight to Las Vegas was scheduled to land around midnight. Her phone began vibrating. She looked at it and noticed that it was Rico. He was just on his way to sleep, but before he went, he wanted to say good night and inform her that he would be attending the court proceedings in the morning.

Before he could get a word in, she called him a liar. "You were supposed to be here two days ago to reveal to me and your children this so-called glamorous lifestyle we were about to be living. I knew you were lying! I can't stand your azz!"

"So Mrs. Vena hadn't called you yet? he asked.

"She did, but I told her to call me back. I was getting my hair braided when she called."

Rico shook his head in frustration. It was no use trying to explain. "I'll call you in the morning," he said before hanging up.

Once again, as bad as he wanted to leave he couldn't. His wife had every reason to feel the way she did in addition to the added pressure of having to deal with her court situation. "In just a matter of time," he thought to himself before turning off his lights...

The next morning, he was up and out of the door and on his way to the Las Vegas municipal courthouse. When he arrived, he noticed it was packed to capacity. He also noticed that the Las Vegas Daily Press was there taking pictures. He took a seat behind his wife and her law team. He noticed that Tamia was talking with her lawyer, but she seemed distraught. When the court proceedings, began her lawyer stood up and told the judge that his client Tamia Dallas wanted to recant her previous statement.

The ohs and ahs in the courtroom were heightened as flashes from the press cameras began taking pictures. The judge banged his gavel, "ORDER IN THE COURT! ORDER IN THE COURT! This proceeding shall remain in order. There will be no more outbursts, or you will be asked to exit my courtroom immediately!"

The judge looked at Tamia and asked if she was coerced. She responded no. He asked was she promised anything. She replied no. He then, asked if she could read and write. She agreed.

"Let the record state that Tamia Dallas has willingly chosen to recant her previous statement on the defendant's behalf."

"What the hell!" Rico said.

He sat up straight he wanted to hear this, just as much as everyone else in the courtroom.

Tamia stood up to address the court. She looked back and noticed Rico looking her directly in her eyes. She took several deep breaths and she began to explain. She said the sex that she and Tasha had with both defendants was consensual and that her rape allegations against them were false. She stated that even though they killed her best friend, she couldn't allow them to be charged with rape. She just couldn't live with that on her conscious.

Rico couldn't believe the words he was hearing out of his wife's mouth. Here he was breaking his neck to prove his faithfulness, while his wife was having an orgy in a Vegas hotel. With that thought boiling in his mind, he got up and stormed out of the courthouse. Immediately, he wanted to divorce her, but he knew he couldn't just react from his feelings. He knew he had to think his way through the chaos. He was aware that the enemy was working hard, not only on him, but he was targeting his family as well. Rico went straight to his Ceasers Palace dining room area to meditate and to ask for universal guidance. Afterward, he got dressed. He had another meet and greet before the show.

Back In The United Kingdom...

James, Vena, and Lamont had found their next prospect. He was a twenty-two-year-old British dancer named Malachi. He stood six feet even and weighed around 220 pounds of pure muscle. His energy was amazing. He was handsome, charming, energetic, and dedicated to his craft. Three months ago, he was hand-picked by James himself just in case Xavier didn't make the cut. The entire time James was teaching him the knowledge, wisdom, and understanding of the secret, the 48 laws of power, and the art of

seduction. He was being groomed the entire time to become a part of the brotherhood.

James also knew about Rico's wife and all of the chaos she had going on over in the States. He wanted to see just how Rico was going to handle it before he granted him his official retirement. Rico's hard work, dedication, and love of the craft were never in question. His level of consciousness was.

Rico was backstage when a woman entered wearing an, I love Jackhammer Slim t-shirt, but this time, she had a VIP pass. Her hair was done differently, but her walk looked too familiar. It was none other than Yancey herself.

"I don't know if you remember me, but I am the woman who tried to blackmail you for 5 million dollars. I came to apologize. I was all in my head at the time and desperate times cause for desperate measures, but I'm truly one of your biggest fans. No worries, this can be our little secret," she winked and walked away.

Yancey was never there to look at Rico's real estate properties. She was there to look at Rico and to study him. The entire time they were in the Dominican Republic, she purposely lagged just to see how he walked. She observed his body structure and his aura.

She had been a fan too long not to know who he was. She even noticed that he didn't wear any jewelry. That was definitely not the Rico she was accustomed to seeing. What sealed the deal for her was when he refused to have sex with her. She had never in her twenty-seven years of life met a straight, or married man, with that much discipline to deny her sex, especially standing half naked. It takes someone used to that kind of pressure and from her 48-hour personal assessment, she was totally convinced, that Rico was Jackhammer Slim.

Rico couldn't focus on what just happened because he was devastated and heartbroken. He hadn't loved a woman the way he loved Tamia Dallas. The thought of another man having unadulterated sex with his wife made him angry. Loyalty is something he proudly stood on and the fact that she violated that trust was shocking. He wanted to forgive her, but an orgy? The things he was imagining were getting him more depressed. He knew Satan was trying to take advantage of his thoughts in his weakest moment. So, without further or adieu, he began to apply the universal knowledge that was taught to him. The law of attraction states that you can control any situation once you have control over yourself.

Rico went straight into his meditation ritual. For the next hour, he exhaled all of his negative energy and thoughts and he inhaled positive frequencies in order to think his way through the chaos. After a solid hour, he felt amazing. Tonight, he only had a ten o'clock show to perform and the mission was to go out there and to give the people who they came to see.

Unbeknownst to him Vena, James, and Lamont would be attending the show. Rico burst onto the stage with a burst of energy. The women began going insane, as Nelly's, "Hot in Here," hit single blast through the speakers. Rico spotted a beautiful well-proportioned woman sitting front and center. He motioned for her to come up by shining his red light on her. She approached the stage and was blindfolded. Then, she took a seat in his famous red velvet chair. He pulled out a single rose, and a box of chocolate-covered strawberries, while he began walking circles around her chair. Then he started bumping and grinding the chair as if it were her. He gently grabbed her face with his left hand and bit into the strawberry. With his right hand, he leaned forward and began feeding her the strawberry from out of his mouth as the two kissed. The audience went into an all-out frenzy.

The young woman in the chair couldn't see, but she could hear the reactions from the crowd. Her excitement showed by her stomping her heels. Then, he opened her hands and poured body oil into them. He turned towards the crowd and began ripping his shirt to shreds exposing his well-chiseled six-pack, while licking his tongue out in a provocative manner. He turned towards the woman in the chair and allowed her to rub his body down with oil. She didn't hesitate to caress everything she could. She even grabbed his man-meat. He'd never let a woman cross that line before, but tonight, he was giving the people what they wanted. The crowd of twenty-five hundred women exited the theater conversing and excited about another lit performance from The World-Famous Jackhammer Slim.

From the look of it, Rico ended his show with a bang. James and the crew thoroughly enjoyed seeing their protégé put that work in. Whatever he had going through in his and in his personal life wasn't affecting him while he was on the stage, because he handled business, with grace, style, and professionalism. That was James' sole purpose for attending tonight. He needed to know if Rico could apply the knowledge during his weakest moments and still be able to perform to the best of his ability.

"The brand was respected, protected, and honored tonight!!" James said proudly.

Rico's show went viral. It was a groundbreaking performance that was talked about and shared over the internet by millions. He didn't know it yet, but that would be his last performance as The World-Famous Jackhammer Slim.

Malachi was back at his Ceasers Palace suite watching Rico's performance live on his phone. He realized he had some big shoes to fill, but he felt as if he was up for the challenge. This was his first time in the United States. He was thousands of miles away from his family and friends back home in London. He knew very much about the harvest that was promised if he stayed the course and followed the blueprint. He was honored to be able to see Rico's final curtain close. Now, it was time for him to blaze his trail, and leave his personal mark as The World-Famous Jackhammer Slim, just as others before him had. He stood on his balcony overlooking the bright lights of Sin City with his mask on.

"Get ready, because it's about to be a bloody showdown in Vegas!" he yelled.

Meanwhile, in the penthouse, Rico received a surprise knock at his door. Big Will answered and all you heard was people joking about how tall he was.

"Man, you all have to get some better tall jokes," he said laughing.

Rico heard the commotion and exited his master suit dressed in his Versace robe and slippers. "What a pleasant surprise," he said smiling from ear to ear. He hadn't seen James and Lamont since his trip to London months ago.

"And a surprise well worth giving," James replied. "Rico, what a journey. You came to us a young energetic talent. Unfortunately, you fell short of my expectations, but you were determined to prove to us that you were not your mistakes. You bit the bullet and held yourself accountable for your ways, thoughts, and actions. We took notice and decided to give you a second chance.

Ever since, you've done nothing more than make us proud to call you our brother for life. Thank you for believing in the process. You stood through the challenges by applying the knowledge given to you. For that alone, I'm forever grateful."

Rico stood there wondering what was happening. "So, you saying all this to say?" He stood there as if he had a clue.

Everyone burst out laughing. That's when Vena broke the ice and said, "You can FINALLY hang your jersey up in the rafters."

Rico was so overwhelmed that he just stood shocked. "Thank you for the opportunity. It's been one helluva ride, but I wouldn't take it back for anything!"

FINALLY

The all-white Mercedes 2024 G-wagon pulled into the driveway of Tamia's parent's house. Rico stepped out smelling like Versace Blue Jeans cologne. Sporting over a hundred thousand dollars in jewelry. His drip was an all-black and red Balmain hoodie, a pair of black Armani bandana jeans, and a fresh pair of black and red Jordan 4s. Everything about him said he was rich as hell. Onyx was the first person to see his father. Immediately, he ran over and began hugging him. Rico looked up and noticed Tamia and her mother standing on the porch.

"Can I get some love?" he asked Tamia.

She walked down from the porch slowly, but he could tell she really missed him. They embraced and kissed for minutes. Rico loved his wife with everything in him and he couldn't wait to reveal his long-awaited secret to her. First, he had to take her back to their home.

The estate was breathtaking. The 5,347 square foot, seven-bedroom, five-and-and-a-half bathroom white mansion, sitting in the heart of Las Vegas just minutes away from the famous Caesars Palace. Tamia recalled visiting this estate the first day she and Tasha arrived in Vegas. She began recalling it to Rico as they were passing through his security gate. They were welcomed by their two butlers and three maids who were all standing along the driveway when they arrived.

Tamia thought the Maybach Mercedes was something special, until she saw the motorcade of Rolls Royce, BMWs, and Mercedes Benzs that were lined up in his driveway.

"So, you telling me those cars belong to you?" she asked while exiting the vehicle and looking him in the face.

"No, they don't belong to me! They belong to us!" he replied.

He began introducing Tamia to his staff. "This beautiful soul here is Loretta. She can cook a mean gumbo. She loves to sew and do word puzzles in her spare time. Carla is her daughter. She's death, but she can read lips very well. She keeps this estate immaculately flawless.

Rain is her adopted niece. She loves animals and being outside. She's in charge of the landscaping. These two gentlemen here are Winston, our house butler, and Charlie, our driver. Everyone meet the long-awaited Queen of the estate, my beautiful wife, Tamia Dallas."

They each greeted Tamia as she began walking through the door of the estate. It was a breathtaking sight to see. As soon as she entered, she was blown away by the vaulted ceilings and the high arch beams. The golden chandeliers hung fifteen feet above. She hadn't even seen the rest of the house and had already said she was in love with it.

"This is the first house. We actually own three," Rico said as they began their grand tour.

"Three houses bae?"

"Yes and one of them is twice as big as this one. It's our vacation home in California. The other one is in Dove Landing in Chesapeake, VA."

I'm still blown away. This is entirely too much to take in all at once," she replied.

"So, imagine me having all of this and not being able to tell you?" he said laughing.

"You still haven't told me how you accumulated your wealth," she said.

"How about I do you one better and show you," he said. "But that's going to be later!"

Tamia looked at him and said, "You better not be in the Illuminati!"

Rico couldn't help it. He had to laugh.

"Dinner was amazing," Tamia said while still in shock that she was actually living in a mansion while getting serviced hand and foot. She didn't have to lift a finger. "I think I can get used to this baby," she said.

Loretta walked over and began pouring them both a glass of vintage Chateau Petrus 1999, in which she retrieved from their massive wine cellar. They sat and began a beautiful conversation sitting by the fireplace, listening to the crackling sound of the cedar and maple wood burning, and feeling the warmth and coziness of the fire. October London's hit single, "Back To Your Place," played softly in the background. By their fifth glass, they couldn't keep their hands off of one another.

Eventually, they got up and entered their master bedroom where they continued where they left off. Instead of making love on their king-size bed, they settled for the plush nylon carpet, directly in front of the fireplace. The following morning, Rico woke up at the crack of dawn. He began washing his face and brushing his teeth. Minutes later, he walked back into his master bedroom, only to see that Tamia was up staring at him and smiling.

"Damn! I must have put in some serious work last night the way you're standing there smiling at me."

"Boy, shut up!" she responded. "And yes, you definitely did your thing, but I thought you were retired. It's four in the morning."

"I am retired, sweetheart. Last night, was my final night." He looked over at Tamia and she still had the biggest grin on her face. "Damn," Rico said shaking his head. "Well, the only thing that will take me from you now is me waking up early to run. I have to remain and stay physically fit. I'm just going to jog a couple of blocks. I should be back in like twenty minutes," he said while brushing his teeth.

Rico exited the bathroom and noticed Tamia standing in a tight sweatsuit outfit with a pair of Air Max 95. "I want to go out jogging with you," she said making her way to the bathroom.

"You sure?" he asked. "I'm jogging at least a mile."

"You just said a couple of blocks a minute ago, baby," she wined.

"It's not that long. We're running there and riding back."

"Okay! I'm down," she said excitedly while she put her beats by Dre on top of her braids.

Rico looked over at Tamia and thought to himself how amazing it felt, to be with his wife again.

The scenery was epic. The Nevada desert was a sight for sore eyes as the two lovers ran side by side, while their driver, Charlie, lagged behind in their midnight black Rolls Royce Phantom. This was the manifestation of his hard work and dedication. This was, indeed, his bountiful harvest. When they made it back to the mansion Tamia and Rico got prepared to go out. He wanted to take Tamia on a long awaited shopping spree that sshe deserved. He told her he had been waiting to see her fill the walk-in closet.

They arrived to The Shops at Crystals on the Vegas strip, a designer outlet mall, that carried Gucci, Prada, Channel, Cartier, Hermes, North America, Tom Ford, Tiffany & Co. and Louis Vuitton. Several saleswomen tried their absolute hardest to sell Tamia designer dresses, purses, and a sexy pair of red-bottom Louis Vuitton heels, which Rico encouraged her to purchase. After twenty minutes of looking around, Tamia just wasn't feeling the clothing or the sky-high ridiculous prices. She walked over to Rico and said, "Baby, I'm so grateful that we can afford this type of living, but I'm just a round-the-way girl. I'd rather spend the money charging for one outfit, on six."

"So, where to then?" he asked.

She looked at him and said, "Take me to the damn mall!"

He smirked at her request and instructed Charlie to head over to the airport. He texted Vena to see if one of the company's private jets were still in Vegas. She returned his call and said one was available, and that he could head over, but it was going to be around an hour and a half before the pilot arrived.

Rico and Tamia decided to take that time to go and renew their vows. They arrived shortly, at the Little Vegas Wedding Chapel, around noon. The wait was no longer than 15 minutes. Once in, the ceremony took place immediately as the two stood face-to-face along with the pastor. Tamia seemed nervous. Rico held her hand and kissed it. She looked him directly in his eyes and said, "From this day forward, your joy is my joy. Your problems are my problems. Your heart is my heart. Your dreams are my dreams. Your life is our life and I promise to love you unconditionally and to be devoted to you, for the remainder of my life. For better or for worse."

Rico stood there smiling like a kid at Christmas. He took out the vows he'd written down earlier while they waited, and began reading.

"With my whole heart, I promise to remain devoted to you and to continue to grow with you in mind and spirit. To practice patience, kindness, and understanding. I vow to love and to cherish you, for as long as we both shall live."

Seconds later, he pulled out a flawless 15-carat emerald-cut diamond ring, from his back right pocket, that literally took her breath away. They kissed and thanked the pastor before exiting.

Back in their Rolls Royce, Tamia couldn't stop looking at the size of her ring. She had so many thoughts rummaging through her mind because Rico had yet to reveal to her, what he did to earn his finances and that was vital to their marriage. She began doing the math in her head trying to come up with her own estimation of his assets. After, she came to the conclusion, without a doubt in her mind, that Rico was a multi-millionaire.

She began asking herself if he was trying to buy her into not even caring where his finances derived from. Was she being tempted? If so, she definitely wasn't having that. Being raised a devoted Christian she began quoting bible verses in her head. She knew that Satan tried to tempt Jesus. He promised him all of the kingdoms of the world in return for worshipping him. "For what shall it profit a man, if he shall gain the whole world, and lose his own soul," she thought to herself while looking over at her husband. It was that or she was convinced he'd got caught up in the underworld of Sin City and became a part of the Illuminati. She asked God to protect her from the raft of the enemy, and she began to pray silently.

Rico's harvest was so bountiful that even his wife couldn't believe it. The amazing part about it was the fact that he earned, saved, and invested his money. He practiced a cunning lifestyle. Being afforded free food, shelter, and transportation for five years, allowed him to earn an estimated income of over 20 million dollars.

The jet awaited their arrival, Rico's Maybach pulled up ten feet away from it as he and Tamia exited their vehicle and boarded. Three hours later, they landed at JFK International Airport. Rico knew Tamia had never been to New York, and he looked forward to her having the time of her life, which she did.

Back At The Estate

Rico and Tamia relaxed after their long shopping extravaganza. This was the first time she was able to go on an unlimited shopping spree. When they exited the jet, it was epic. Their driver awaited their arrival in the Maybach, while Loretta, Carla, and Winston, were all parked in his motorcade of luxury vehicles. One by one, they entered the jet and would leave off with merchandise to load in each vehicle. For Tamia, this feeling was surreal on all levels.

Back at the estate, Loretta arrived with the Champagne. Rico decided to call his entire staff into the great room to join them for a toast. Once everyone arrived, they held their glasses up while he began. "May the most you wish for, be the least you get. May good fortune precede love and walk with you, and good friends follow you. May this home be a place where friends meet, family gathers, and love grows. May the roof above us never fall in and may we, as friends and family, never fall out." He raised his glass and said, "To the good life."

Everyone followed in unison repeating, "To the good life!" They all drank their champagne and everyone went back to their work assignments.

That's when Rico decided this was the perfect moment. He walked over and began kissing on Tamia. "Baby, I think it's about time I show you what I know you've been dying to see," he said laughing. He knew his wife hadn't fully embraced their amazing blessing because she hadn't as to fly their children over. He asked her to have a seat and told her that he would be returning shortly.

Ten minutes later, a Masked man walked into their great room. At first, he startled her, but once she recognized it was Rico, she began laughing.

"Bae, why are you being so silly? Why do you have Jackhammer Slim's mask? Are you about to strip for me? I got them bands now! Let me see something!" she said while fanning a thick wad of hundreds back in forth in her hand while sticking her tongue out.

Rico stood in character, not saying one word. Suddenly, 50 Cents, "Candy Shop," began blasting from their entertainment system. He walked away and reappeared with his famous red chair.

"You even have the velvet chair bae? Okkkaaaay!" Tamia yelled over the music.

She still hadn't caught on. She began dancing in the chair in a snake motion, moving her head from side to side, while snapping her fingers. Still, she thought it was just a regular costume and that he was just setting the mood for the foreplay.

Suddenly, he leaned over and began nibbling on her left ear. In that minute, she inhaled his cologne, and her legs began shaking nervously. That's when she knew, he was the same person she was on the stage with at Ceasers Palace. Rico didn't even have to say anything. The surprised look in her eyes told him, everything he needed to know. For the next 30 minutes, he performed for his wife, and it was the show of a lifetime.

Tamia was at a loss for words. How and when were just two of many questions she needed answered. After their two-hour-long conversation, she now understood why Rico kept it such a secret.

"But for all of this?" she said while waving her hand, "You better had kept your damn mouth shut!" she said laughing.

Rico felt as if an elephant had just lifted off of his shoulders. He promised his wife that she would never have to work another day. This was something he always wanted to be able to do for her. She thanked him, but said she didn't want to just sit around a big-ass mansion doing nothing. So, Rico agreed to hire her to as his real estate agent. She gladly accepted.

Just outside of their mansion, approximately thirty yards away, Yancey sat in a black tinted-out Yukon snapping photos. The Panasonic Lumix G7 digital night vision camera, she purchased took the best quality pictures and videos. She snapped over fifty crystal clear photos. She knew she had him this time, and there was no way he could get around it. Yancey figured Rico would deny it, but the proof was in the pudding. She decided to text him several pictures of him performing in his great room. Rico received the text and opened it up.

CHAPTER 8

The following day, the couple flew their children in from Virginia. Onyx and Aja had no idea what they were about to experience. Tamia and Rico met them at the McCarran International Private Airport. Onyx and Aja exited the jet excited to see their mother and father standing together. They ran over as fast as they could to embrace them.

"Mommy, me and Onyx were the only ones on the plane," Aja said.

"Did you enjoy your first plane ride?"

"Yes," she replied. "I can't wait to fly back home."

"Well, unfortunately baby, you won't be going back to Grannie's for awhile."

"Why not?" she asked looking up at Tamia.

"Because your father purchased us a beautiful home here in Las, Vegas and I promise you're going to love it."

They all entered the luxury Maybach and headed to their luxurious estate that they could now call home.

This Bitch

Rico laughed at the boldness of Yancey.

"This bitch is determined to get some money out of me," he said to himself while calling her back.

"Hello!?" she answered.

"What type of time, are you on? I'm having a little foreplay with my wife and you trespassing on my property and taking pictures of the shit?

"I know your Jackhammer Slim," she said.

"Jackhammer who?"

"You heard me. Now, you have twenty-four hours to come up with the five million. If not, I'm going to expose who you are, to my two million viewers. If that don't get their attention, your pictures will somehow get leaked to the internet, in which they will probably go viral. So, the cat's out of the bag. Either way, I'm going to get paid. I think it would work out better for you if you just paid me the damn money, Rico! You know damn well, I know your Jackhammer Slim, "she said laughing.

"What I do know is that you're delusional as hell and a stalker," Rico said. "I have the best lawyers on my payroll. You're about to catch a Fed case out here fuckin' with me!" he yelled hanging up in her ear.

Thankfully his wife and children were away school shopping because he was in an all-out rage. Negative thoughts began running rapidly through his mind. Yancey was trying to destroy everything he worked so hard for. This bountiful harvest that James told him he would ride off into the sunset was clearly in jeopardy once again. He felt as if he couldn't catch a break. He thought of several people he could call to make Yancey disappear for a fraction of what she was blackmailing him for. He knew he needed to calm down and think his way through this chaotic mess. He needed advice and that's when he made the call to James.

After explaining over fifteen minutes, how Yancey was on her personal tirade to expose the brotherhood again, James calmly sat and listened. He waited patiently for Rico to finish before he began to talk. "Your life doesn't get easier because you have money. In fact, it gets harder, and not everyone can handle it. That's why it takes a Jackhammer Slim with a mindset and discipline like yourself to navigate his way through the chaos on the stage as well is off. What you learned over the past five years was your preparation for life after Jackhammer Slim. Your problems never stopped, they just enhanced. Like biggie said, 'Mo' money, Mo' problems.' They say it takes a village, but we're a village of men who are thinkers and we never bend, fold, or react. Your problems become my problems and the same with Malachi. We will be taking on every obstacle that comes to or near him. Protecting our brand is vital. As long as we have our brotherhood and positivity running in our veins, we can conquer anything this chaotic world throws our way. Now, give me all the details on Yancey, along with a contact number. I can handle it from here."

Rico couldn't do anything, but sit and wait. He left it in the hands of the big homie. He knew James didn't want any negative attention he was probably going to just write her a check for some millions.

Six Months Later...

Malachi was premiering at the coliseum at Caesars Palace to a sold-out venue of 4100 in the crowd, but tonight was different because it was a Jackhammer Slim presents affair. This meant that Malachi would be sharing the stage with other exotic dancers showcasing their newest talent. So, men and women graced the stands with anticipation. Everyone was said to be attending to support their newest members. Lamont, James, Rico, Tamia, Vena, Big Will, and even his Uncle Ellison, were all there.

Just as expected, Malachi burst out onto the stage full of the energy that only a twenty-year-old could possess. His Jackhammer Slim ensemble was stylish. He wore leather gloves and leather skinny pants. The women seemed to notice it right away. All you heard were screams and cheers throughout his entire performance. During his ten-minute intermission, Vena walked onto the stage and thanked everyone for their support. She also wanted to introduce another one of their newest talents.

The lights cut off and were back on. Within a matter of seconds, there stood a woman. She appeared to be around five foot two, 188- pounds of pure curves, in an all-red leather bodysuit. She was wearing a pair of six-inch knee-high leather boots, along with a red sexy mask that covered her entire head and face. Her long silky ponytail protruded down her back out from the mask. The reaction from the men in the audience was absolutely epic.

Vena approached the microphone and made the announcement. She said, "Ladies and gentlemen, Jackhammer Slim Presents is proud to introduce our newest member The Lady Empress Dancehall Queen. Everyone stood up in awe watching as she strutted the stage with perfection and sexiness. The song, "Hrs and Hrs," by Muni Long, played in the background. She squatted at the end of the stage and signaled, with her long signature nails, for the older gentleman in the audience with a red hat to come up onto the stage. She guided the gentleman over to have a seat. Her entire set was sexy and sensual. She sat him down and began walking in circles around him while sexually swaying her thick curvaceous hips. Then, she stood directly in front of him and went down into a perfect split. The crowd went into an all-out frenzy. She ended it by sitting in his lap and grinding back and forth as if they were having unadulterated sex. She left the man completely speechless.

Suddenly, the music changed into reggae and The Lady Empress set the roof on fire with her seductive dance hall moves, showing her talented dancing skills, and taking over the show. She had the entire building winding and twerking. It was another epic moment for the books. James and Vena looked at each other in approval as they witnessed the amazing energy she brought to the arena. The Lady Empress exited the stage and Malachi entered. He wasn't finished by far. He went back out and ended the show with an amazing performance. Not only did he bring the house down, but he solidified his place in the brotherhood.

Out of curiosity, Rico looked over at Vena and asked, who was The Lady Empress and where did she come from?

She smiled and said, "You will find out when everyone else does."

He gave her the "really" look. She smirked and said, "I'm just the messenger."

Two weeks later, everyone was asked to meet up at James' Vegas estate to have a welcoming ceremony for the newest members, Malachi and The Lady Empress. For the past two weeks, both names had been buzzing all over Vegas and every social media outlet. The Jackhammer Slim brand was evolving with the times by recruiting a younger generation of talented males and females.

Rico was late, due to traffic. When he finally arrived to the estate, he noticed the usual motorcade of Maybach's which was normal, but one of them stuck out and caught his attention. This Maybach was a newer one. It was painted Barbie pink with a white leather interior. Rico asked the chauffeur whose vehicle it belonged to. and he replied back that it belonged to its owner.

"Perfect answer!" he said making his way into the exclusive mansion.

When the door opened, Mr. Ellison stood welcoming him. Rico noticed it wasn't a gathering, but a celebration. It had to be over a hundred and fifty people in attendance. There was food, champagne, and unlimited entertainment. Rico went straight over to the food caterer and had him stack his plate with BBQ chicken, beef ribs, baked macaroni and cheese, collard greens, candied yams, and deviled eggs. The minute he turned around he noticed Yancey and dropped his entire plate on the floor.

"Bitch, you got a lot of nerve coming up in my people's shit. You done messed up for real this time."

Yancey didn't say one word, as a matter of fact, she nonchalantly began making her a plate of food. Rico hurried back with James, Big Will, and Lamont, while she was sitting down eating her food without a care in the world. James looked at Rico and said, "Say hello to The Lady Empress!"

Rico didn't know how to respond because, over the past several months, she had been nothing but a headache. "But why?" he asked James.

They excused themselves and went off into the theater room. It was there they could talk in private. James said, "I decided to recruit Yancey because she had a burning desire in her to be successful. After having a long talk with her and getting to know intimate details about her life, I knew she was exactly the person I wanted to have as a part of this beautiful movement. She's special, loyal, and dedicated. I think we're going to make a lot of money with her. She's going to change the game for generations to come, just as you have. We all have some good in us. It just takes the right person or persons to bring it out. I believe, outside of her extortion methods, she's a cool down-to-earth woman. You two were friends at one time, correct?"

"Yes, we were. Until she thought she penned me."

"Unfortunately, I have to say she did. She told me that nobody could convince her, except Jesus, that you weren't Jackhammer Slim. She was willing to go to bat for her money. So, with that being said, I decided to give her the opportunity of a lifetime and she gladly accepted the million-dollar bonus under our non-disclosure agreement."

A knock was at the door and it was Vena and Yancey. Yancey walked over and apologized to Rico for trying to extort him... again. He laughed and accepted her apology with a big hug.

"Now, let's all get back to the party!" James said.

Their friends and associates in the real estate and business world began dispersing by 1 am. The only people left were the brotherhood. James told everyone to walk with him because he needed some fresh air. They exited the estate and James began to talk. "From this day forward it's family over everything. Yancey, you witnessed firsthand how important this legacy is. What we have created is a legal hustle that consists of wealth, fortune, and financial freedom, but only if you apply the rules. Yancey and Malachi, what you are amongst is a core group of black successful multimillionaires. The same opportunity they were given, has now been afforded to you. All of this can and will be yours in five years. Stay focused, stay positive, grind harder than you ever have in your life, and I promise you, the world will be your oyster. With that being said, welcome to the brotherhood!"

They all entered their luxury company Maybach's leaving the estate and going their separate ways. James and Vena headed over to the airport where their private jet awaited their arrival. James had enough of being in the US. He was ready to get back to his estate in the United Kingdom. He missed everything about London, including talking with his British accent, along with drinking his favorite combination of morning breakfast tea with milk and sugar. He missed dipping his crackers and crumpets into it, while reading the Daily Sun.

"In just a matter of hours, I'll be back home," he said to himself staring out of the window.

Rico went back home to Norfolk, VA and started his nonprofit organization. There, he opened a youth outreach center where kids could go and escape the street gang violence and senseless shootings that occurred daily in their community. The outreach center included a laundry mat where kids could bring their clothes to wash for free. He also had a beauty and barber shop where boys could get a free haircut twice a month, and girls could get their hair done anytime. He also had a cafeteria where he provided free lunch and snacks six days a week. He funded their field trips twice a month to Bush Gardens, Kings Dominion, and various professional football and basketball games. All he asked was for their commitment which included staying away from drugs and gangs. They also had to graduate from high school. Once they graduated, he promised he would pay their college tuition in full. That was his personal commitment to giving back to his community and to the universe.

Malachi was back at his Caesars Palace residency after another jaw-dropping performance. Now, he could finally take his mask off and breathe. He walked out onto his balcony to enjoy the fresh Vegas night air. He looked out into the bright lights of Sin City with hopes and dreams of doing it bigger than the ones who came before him.

Yancey decided to drive home to Virginia for the holidays to surprise her brothers. She'd recently found out where they were located through a friend of a friend. She was told that her brothers were both doing well and that the eldest was a rising track star. She also heard that Chris, her youngest brother, was a prominent drum major at Norfolk State University. Hearing the good news about them both made her proud.

She pulled up to her brother's apartment building in her luxury pink and white Maybach. She stepped out looking like the celebrity she was. She instructed her driver to knock on the apartment door. Seconds later, she recognized a male walking out looking in her direction. "Wow! Look how big he's gotten," she said to herself. He stood there looking as if he had not a clue to who she was. That's when she took her Chanel designers off and yelled, "Boy if you don't get your juice box head ass down here!"

He'd heard that joke a time or two, and suddenly he yelled back, "Evette, is that you Sis?"

"Yes, it is!"

He ran down the stairs and swept her off of her feet because he was so excited to see her.

"Where is Donte?" she asked.

"He's the manager at the Wendy's on Monticello. He should be off... unless he's doing overtime."

"Well, get in. We are going to pick him up. You've gotten so big Christopher," she said looking at his mature face. "I see you went and grew you some muscles. You even have some peach fuzz on top of your lip," she said.

Chris began laughing. "I'm almost nineteen, Sis. I'ma grown man now! You look different too! I remember you being skinny as a broomstick." She burst out laughing.

The Wendy's was five minutes away so Yancey and Christopher took that time to catch up a little. When they arrived, Christopher exited the vehicle to get their brother Donte. Minutes later, he too burst through the door excited to see his sister. She hugged them both and began to cry. Suddenly, they all began crying. It was an emotional moment, for them all. This was the first time they had been together since the death of their mother almost a decade ago.

Once in, she instructed her driver to drive them to the Virginia Beach oceanfront. She was convinced that would give her enough time to discuss everything with her siblings. They had so many questions, and by the time they arrived at the oceanfront, she'd already answered a majority of them.

Two weeks later…

With a brand-new lease on life, Yancey was able to move her brothers from out of their poverty-stricken apartment complex to a condo just off of 21st and Atlantic. She also brought them new vehicles. She purchased little Chris a BMWx7 and Donte a Range Rover Sport SUV. She even opened them both bank accounts at Capital One.

By the end of their all-out blessing, her eldest brother asked what was her means of acquiring such wealth. She laughed and told him as much as she would love to tell him, she couldn't. Eventually, she would tell him everything when the time was right. The hardest part was her breaking their hearts by telling them she was going away, again, to create a better life for them. She knew they wouldn't understand. She promised them that their harvest was on its way.

"Just believe me. I got us. Call me anytime," she said while entering her Maybach and pulling off into the Norfolk city nightlife.

Yancey cried the entire ride, but she vividly remembered what James had told her. He said, "Even though you will be able to afford all the luxuries life can offer, this lifestyle gets lonely. In order to receive your harvest, you're going to have to be willing to sacrifice. He said that the unwritten law in becoming The Lady of Empress Dance Hall Queen is to forever remain a mystery. You can never expose your identity to anyone including your closest family members. Not only will you retire, but you will be able to retire a multi-millionaire and will be able to ride off into the sunset with peace of mind while enjoying your bountiful harvest...knowing you did it the right way."

She smiled knowing everything he was telling her was factual. It was right before her eyes so, she had to believe it. Suddenly, she cleaned her face and put her makeup on. She was headed to the airport where her luxury private jet awaited her arrival. Five hours and thirty-five minutes later, her flight was about to land. She hurried and put her mask on. She knew paparazzi hung out at private air scripts.

As soon as she exited her jet, cameras began flashing and fans were screaming and asking for autographs. Her driver and security detail were all there waiting at the moment she arrived. She was placed in another Maybach and was driven away in a six-car motorcade on her way to perform at yet, another sold-out venue, the Jamaican Sumfest in Montego Bay Jamaica.

Jamaican Sumfest in Montego Bay Jamaica.

A lot of her favorite dancehall artists she admired growing up were backstage asking to take pictures with her. This was so surreal. She never imagined she would be this big of a superstar, but then again, she never doubted herself either. She stood backstage taking it all in. She could hear the roaring crowd chanting her name. This was everything she ever dreamed of and =]this was her moment.

"Ladies and gentlemen, introducing The World-Famous, Lady of Empress......

As usual, she tore the main stage down. Once backstage, she hurried and changed her attire. Minutes later, she emerged back out as Yancey and walked through the crowd without a care in the world. She exited out of the main door, and into the crowd cheering as she watched and enjoyed the rest of the show alongside the sold-out arena.

www.ingramcontent.com/pod-product-compliance
Lightning Source LLC
Chambersburg PA
CBHW071431300726
48976CB00004B/1302